Colette

Michelina Vinter

Disclaimer

Any resemblance to any live or dead individual is purely unintentional and coincidental.

ISBN-13: 978-0-9891102-0-4

ISBN-10: 0989110206

DEDICATION

I dedicate this book to my grandparents, Raymonde Vinter, Roger Vinter, Michelina Zambelli, and Antoine Zambelli, who never hesitated to give of their time to help me grow and thrive.

ACKNOWLEDGMENTS

While this novel is a work of fiction, I interviewed my grandmother before she passed to get the feel for what life during World War II, and especially life in Paris, was really like. So once again I must thank Raymonde Vinter for her contribution to my work. I also thank my husband, children, and parents for their unrelenting support.

Colette

CHAPTER 1

Paris, Summer 1938

Colette and her friend Anne rushed across the boulevard Saint-Germain. They had just finished their last exam and were finally corporate secretaries. Most young French women would give their left arms to be in their shoes. At eighteen years of age, Colette and Anne had jobs lined up and the world at their feet. After a short walk, they reached the terrace of the Café Saint Michel. They sat down at their favorite table, ordered the aromatic brew so typical of the country, and waited for the students of the Sorbonne to come out in swarms from the old building across the street. Soon the boulevard Saint Michel would be bursting with activity. The cafés' terraces would fill with young people eager to celebrate the onset of summer. There would be singing and maybe dancing. And there would definitely be flirting.

Colette was concentrating on watching a lanky, brown-haired boy holding a checkered flat hat in his hands hurriedly cross the street, when her view was obstructed by a very tall figure. The man in front of her must have been six feet four, at least. He looked very distinguished and not at all at ease in this environment. As a matter of fact, he looked kind of lost. His blond hair was shimmering in the sun, and his angular jaw made him look very masculine. Colette could not quite make out the color of his eyes but decided they must be blue. "What did this man want?" she wondered. At that very moment, he approached her, and in a very approximate French attempted to ask for directions to the Boulinier bookstore, after he introduced himself as Adam Walker. Colette was charmed to hear such an accent and figured that he must be a tourist from the United States of America. Since she was at the top of her class in English, she thought she would help him in his own language and spare him the indignity of having to stumble through the conversation in

French. And instead of explaining to him that he only had to walk toward the boulevard Saint-Germain and stop about three blocks before he reached the Seine River, she opted to take him there herself.

As they walked along the boulevard Saint Michel, Adam could not help but notice that Colette was a very attractive young woman with the most eye-catching attributes. Indeed, not only was she beautiful, with her petite frame, long brown hair, blue eyes, and heart-shaped face, but she also spoke his language. And how refreshing was that? He had not uttered a word of English since he had arrived a few days earlier. This assignment was supposed to be easy; find the book his old colleague needed for his research, purchase the item, and travel back to the University of California at Berkeley, where he could go back to his own teaching. This was really supposed to be a vacation, a few weeks in France, where he could enjoy the women and the wine before going back to a quiet life in sunny California. Instead, he had gotten headache after headache as he realized that his high school French was far from being fluent. Now he knew. His teachers had lied to him. And he smiled to himself.

But this was only his cover. Tonight, he would have to meet with his informant. As a member of the United States intelligence community, Adam had been sent to France to gather information in order to prepare for the possibility of war. The rise to power of Adolph Hitler and the general tension in Europe appeared to be indicating an impending conflict. The United States would want to stay away, but it still needed to evaluate the scope of the problem and the impact on their barely recovering economy. Of course, Adam had to blend in with the French as much as he could during his stay.

But he was not off to a good start. As he was about to cross the street, Colette pulled him back as hard as she could and almost made him lose his balance. He was about to ask her for an explanation when he saw a white Delahaye cabriolet zoom by right where he would have stood, had Colette not interfered with his plan. This sweet little woman had effectively saved his life.

And before he could say a single word, she smiled at him and said, "This is Paris, sir, and French men are mad men on the road. You really need to pay attention if you want to stay alive."

Colette had no idea how right she was. If Adam wanted to stay alive, in his line of work, he needed to be on his toes at all times. There would be no more daydreaming about this woman or anyone else for that matter. He had to stay focused.

Once they reached the bookstore, Colette was entrusted with the title of the book Adam was hunting for, so she could ask the store owner as to its whereabouts. After she learned where the book was located, they walked through the aisles, smelling and looking at all the beautifully decorated masterpieces that lay in front of them. But within minutes, Adam had purchased the old volume he was seeking and was walking out with Colette. He liked her. She was his damsel in shining armor. He liked her so much that he was going to ask her to be his guide for the remainder of his trip. It was a crazy idea, really, not one that would be conducive to much spying. But first he would ask her out to lunch the next day to thank her for all her help.

All too soon, they arrived back at Anne's table. The faithful friend had been holding down the fort by herself and making sure seats were still available for Colette and her potential guest.

The wind had picked up a little, so Colette held her lightly flowing skirt close to her body as she sat down on the chair next to her friend. And when asked if he would sit with them for a while, Adam was more than happy to oblige. He did not want to be left to his own devices so early in the evening. After all, his meeting was not until ten o'clock that night. The sun was still shining, and the air was still warm and breezy as only the best of days can be in Paris. Colette ordered lemonade for herself and a glass of red wine for Adam. Once Adam shared his plans with his young new friend and made his offer, she accepted the job of being his tour guide; after all, she had a few weeks' vacation before her new career would get under way. She would take full advantage of that time and gladly play tourist with the tall, handsome American. She had been right. His eyes were indeed blue, the deepest, most beautiful blue she had ever seen.

***

As Adam was walking back to his hotel on rue de Rivoli, he realized that as smitten as he was by Colette he knew very little about her. How old was she? How many brothers and sisters did she have? Were her parents still alive? Why had she chosen to become a secretary instead of going for a university degree? Did she want to move to the States? Now, where did that last question come from? He had just met the girl for heaven's sake, and she had just become part of his cover. Anyhow, tomorrow, when she picked him up, he would have to ask most of them. He wanted and needed to know everything about her. And in spite of the wonderfully mellowing wine he had ingested in her presence, he knew that tonight, he would not find sleep easily.

He finally reached the corner of the rue de Rivoli and rue du Louvre. He was to meet a young Frenchman named Richard, and would acquire the file he needed to do a thorough analysis, which he would then present to Franklin D. Roosevelt in person within the next couple of months. This file represented essential intelligence gathered from many European countries over the last six months. He had been told that his contact was fluent in at least five languages and that he was able to pass as a citizen of at least as many countries. Once the exchange was made, Adam headed back to his hotel.

Soon enough he reached his destination, He asked for the key to his room and went straight up so the clerk would not start a pointless conversation. He had had enough French for one day and only wanted to go to his room so he could look at his newly acquired file.

To try to calm down, he opted to take a bath. But through the soap suds, all he could see was Colette and her warm, gentle smile. He would count the seconds until he could see her again. And instead of counting sheep, he did just that. It was obviously not a very effective sleep aid, and Adam saw the sunrise before he was able to close his eyes.

***

Colette was walking on air. She would see Adam tomorrow, and the day after, and the day after that, and for the next three weeks. She had taken the metro to the twentieth arrondissement, where her parents lived with her maternal grandparents. She was grinning from ear to ear as she walked in the door of their apartment. She kissed them all to say hello and waltzed to her room. Her little brother, fourteen-year-old Pierre, looked shocked. What had gotten into Colette? She had never acted so dim-witted before. Her twelve-year-old sister, Josette, had a similar expression on her face. And without even consulting each other, both youngsters ran after her. They always wanted to know everything about their older sister's life, and Colette obliged them by regaling them with stories of the day's escapades. But today was special. She wanted to keep this adventure to herself. She felt as if sharing it would make it disappear. So she talked about her exams, her graduation, and her upcoming job. She discussed the singing and the laughing that went on in the cafés and the frenzy with which all the students wanted to celebrate, but she did not utter a word about her striking and oh-so-temporary new boss.

Once she was done with her daily show-and-tell, she put on her cotton nightgown and went straight to bed. She wanted to get her beauty sleep before she met Adam the next day. She fully intended on making him notice her. She wanted her first kiss to be with this man she had just met. She just knew it was going to be special. And unlike the man of her dreams, she fell asleep within seconds.

MICHELINA VINTER

CHAPTER 2

When Colette woke up, everyone was still asleep. Even her grandparents, who generally started their day at dawn, were not out of their room. For once, she would surprise them all and make them black coffee so they could have a fresh cup without having to brew it themselves. After she was done with a breakfast that consisted of a big bowl of café au lait and buttered toast, she washed her hair, ironed her dress, and polished her shoes. By then the house was stirring, and her sister joined her in her room. She had just put on her favorite dress with bouffant sleeves and a well-adjusted waist.

Eager to have her sister's opinion, she asked, "What do you think? Do you like the beautiful flowers on the fabric, or is it too much?"

Before Josette could reply, Pierre, who was passing by Colette's bedroom in his pajamas, teased, "You look like a big flowerpot. Beware of the bees out there!"

Josette said reassuringly to her older sister, "Of course not! You look beautiful, as always!"

And on that note, Colette said good-bye to her family and left for her temporary job. As she walked outside, she thought she should take the subway and head for rue de Rivoli. She was to meet Adam at his hotel so she could accompany him on his Paris discovery.

The trip was not too long, and soon she was waiting for him in the lobby. His arrival took her breath away. The man was just too tall. And his shoulders were just too wide. He was wearing a very proper brown tweed jacket, navy-blue slacks, a blue cotton shirt, and a matching tie. If the weather was going to be any hotter than it had been the previous day, Colette thought that the poor man would surely melt on the spot. She bade him a good morning and pointed him toward the door.

***

12

Adam could not wait to see Colette again. He had barely slept, and so when the sun came up, he was ready to meet her in the lobby. She, of course, did not arrive until a few hours later. She looked young and beautiful in her freshly pressed flower-print dress, with her long hair flowing over her shoulders, her big blue eyes, and her well rested face with her angelic smile. He greeted her with a warm handshake and walked toward the door as she had instructed him.

Once they were on the boulevard, Colette entrusted Adam with her plans for the day. They would first go to the Eiffel Tower and walk on the champ de Mars. They would then have lunch in a bistro by the Seine River and would end the afternoon with a walk in the Luxembourg Gardens. It would be a full and tiring day, but much would be accomplished, and Adam would be satisfied he was getting his money's worth of Paris adventures.

So Colette led him through the maze that eventually got them on the metro and out into the fresh air near the Eiffel Tower. And as they climbed up the iron structure, Adam could see Paris in all its glory. The view was magnificent. From the Sacré Coeur to Notre Dame, he could see all the old buildings that spanned the city. Colette's enthusiasm for her hometown was catching, and Adam soon believed he was looking at the most beautiful town in the world with the most attractive woman he had ever seen.

By the time they walked back down, they were starving. Since the Eiffel Tower was right on the Seine, they were able to get to their restaurant within a few minutes. The place was a typical French bistro where the food was prepared family style by the owner's wife. They ate the dish of the day, a *petit salé aux lentilles*, the only dish served in the establishment, and a dessert of *îles flotantes*. The meal was served with a nice ruby-red wine that mellowed the senses, the kind of wine that would make anyone drinking it want to go for a nap under a tree in a quiet park. But to Adam's great surprise, instead of looking for the most luscious grass under the thickest tree, Colette ordered coffee and asked for the day's newspaper.

They spent the next hour reading and discussing current events. She too had been worried about an upcoming war. She was concerned about Hitler and the fact that European countries were not preparing for a conflict. Granted, they had fought the last war thinking it would indeed be the very last. But hiding their head in the sand regarding Germany's advances toward a conflict was just plain ridiculous, explained Colette. The young lady was more than a pretty face. She was smart, and she understood much more about the intricacies of world politics than most

American young women her age. She was a delight to be around.

Once Adam paid the check, they walked through the Luxembourg Gardens and found a nice tree that would allow them to digest peacefully. They sat down on the grass, and Adam loosened his tie as the day was getting warmer and warmer.

And as he was staring at Colette, wondering what hold this woman had over him, she said, "There is going to be a thunderstorm soon."

"And how do you know that?" replied the young professor.

She answered, a little surprised by the question, "It's obvious. The swallows are flying low. That generally means that a thunderstorm is coming. And that's good because it will clear the air, and tomorrow will be much cooler."

That was music to Adam's ears. He was dying in his tweed jacket and long-sleeved shirt. Thank God he had loosened his tie, but that was only helping a little.

After a nice long rest, they opted not to tempt fate and decided to walk back to Adam's hotel. But about halfway through their journey, the storm Colette had mentioned started throwing buckets of water at them. They decided to run for it, but by the time they reached the front door, they were both soaking wet.

Colette's hair was dripping little beads of water onto her already soaked dress, now clinging to her body. Adam could just make out a hint of skin under the wet fabric. She looked lovely. He really wanted to be a gentleman; he did not want to scare her off. After all, he was ten years older than her. But he wanted her. He wanted her so badly that his whole body ached. So he leaned forward and placed his mouth on hers. To his great surprise, she pulled back instantly and slapped him as hard as she could.

"I don't know what you are doing, but you have got the wrong impression. I am not that kind of girl," she told him in the coldest tone she could muster.

Embarrassed, and cheek burning, Adam apologized profusely: "I don't know what came over me…You looked so lovely. I just wanted to kiss you, to feel your lips on mine. They just seemed so soft. I really did not mean to offend you. Please don't let this incident stop you from being my guide tomorrow. I promise this will never happen again."

***

The next day, and the day after that, and for the whole week, Colette met Adam to help him discover the city she loved so much. They enjoyed having lunch on the Place du Tertre and looking at the artists painting and sketching the various scenes that played out in front of them. Some of the tourists even had their portrait painted on the spot, and one could see that the talent that brewed there was by no means ordinary. And while they walked among the many artists, Adam noticed a man with a beret who was drawing furiously on a napkin. The sketch included a Minotaur, which was rather odd in this environment. However, Adam was riveted to the work of art, and he asked the creator if he could purchase the napkin from him.

The man simply replied, "You like it? Take it. It's just a study for a painting I am working on."

Adam thanked him profusely and left with Colette at his side.

From the Arc de Triomphe to the Louvre, they walked together and talked incessantly. They laughed. They even held hands. And this time Colette did not recoil. She even seemed to really enjoy the physical contact. Adam told Colette about his family. He talked about his five brothers and his baby sister, and he told her about their family home in New York, where his parents still lived with the younger members of the bunch. He talked about his job as a university professor in California, about his life in general, and the fact that his mother was pushing him to give her grandchildren. After all, he was the oldest. He should really marry first. But nowhere in their numerous conversations did Adam mention his other activities.

Colette talked about her family and about how close she was to her grandparents, her cousins, uncles, and aunts, her brother and sister, and her parents. She talked about how they all had dinner together on Sunday nights, when her grandmother cooked their favorite dishes. She talked about the laughter and the easygoing atmosphere that surrounded them all and how much they really loved each other in spite of their occasional arguments.

Adam was touched by her rendition of her family life. He had always thought his family was tight, but it was nothing like that. He could never talk about them with the warmth Colette had shared as she was describing them all.

***

The following weekend, Colette and her friends had planned on going on a picnic by the Marne River, where they would also be able to swim. They were going to stay well into the evening and build a bonfire. Adam had agreed to join them. Pierre and Josette would be there too. It was going to be a day to remember.

The whole gang had decided to meet in front of Colette's house at nine o'clock on Saturday so they could all drive together to a secluded area of the river where they were to spend the day. A young man who looked very familiar walked toward one of the cars and got behind the wheel. Adam could not really make out his face, but the overall shape of his body reminded him of something. The car quickly filled up with the young people who were joining the picnic. He and Colette got in another car, which followed the first. And the whole group drove to the riverbank. They set up their blankets and food as fast as they could, so they could start eating soon. The air was already sizzling and promised to only get hotter. Some of the guys went swimming while the gals sat around and talked. Adam looked positively scrumptious in the swimming trunks he had gotten for the occasion.

Colette did not look so bad herself, in her navy-blue suit. The small skirt that comprised the bottom part of her swimming attire showed off her long legs quite nicely. She went by the riverbank to get the boys' attention so they could come eat, when she noticed that her cousin and Adam were talking.

Colette walked over to them and said, "I see you guys have met. Richard is my cousin and one of the smartest guys I know."

And looking at her cousin, she continued, "Adam is my employer. I have been showing him around the city for the last couple of weeks. He is a professor from the University of California at Berkeley and will be returning home soon."

"He better," mumbled Richard, who did not seem happy with this turn of events.

The young man had always been very protective of his cousin, and the fact that his American contact was courting Colette was making him suspicious. He would have to keep an eye on her and see how things evolved.

After lunch, Colette decided to wait the customary two hours before she joined the boys in the river She described her recent days to Anne, who wanted to hear all the little details of her friend's adventures. Adam, who had no such respect for the two-hour rule, was already in the water and playing ball with the boys. Colette would have loved to join him sooner, but rules were rules. And at that very moment, she hated the rules. When the two hours were up, the young lady dove into the water without hesitation. She was a really good swimmer and enjoyed the feel of the cool water on her skin. The gang always went to the same place on the river, where Mother Nature had created a pool by the side of the riverbed, so they could play all day without worrying about the river's current disturbing their games.

Soon it was time to build the bonfire. They piled some wood they had brought and what they could find in the forest nearby. The evening went as planned. Everyone was enjoying the first days of summer. Some were toasting the occasion a little more than others. Colette had not had any alcohol to drink because she had planned on going swimming again after dinner. However, a young man named Robert had not had the same foresight. And when Colette decided to make good on her plan, the dear boy decided to follow her. She tried to stop him, telling him that he had had too much to drink and should probably not enter the water. But he refused to listen to her and walked right in.

The young woman was swimming peacefully in the middle of the creek when one of her friends yelled, "Colette, I just saw a rat and a couple of snakes in the river."

And since she hated both, Colette decided to head back quickly before she met one of the creatures. But as she started back, she noticed that

Robert was not following her. He appeared to be pretending to drown.

"Stop clowning around, Robert," she shouted.

But the young man took a final plunge and did not come back up. At that very instant, Colette knew that her friend was in big trouble. She swam back toward him and dove where she thought she might have a chance to find him. The water was pitch dark, and she could hardly see. She extended her arms out in front of her, and as if driven by a supernatural force, she collided with him. The next step was to bring him back to shore.

She came back up to the surface and cried for help as she tried to swim back. She was holding Robert in the rescue position she had been taught at school during physical education classes, but he was too heavy. And all she heard from the shore was, "We can't see you. Swim closer."

Colette quickly decided she would not die for this idiot who had not followed her advice, but she would at least do her very best to save his sorry hide. So she started swimming under water as fast as she could while keeping her friend's head out of the water. Whenever she needed a breath, she would come back up for air and let him go under for a second or two. She kept this up until she was near enough for Adam to jump in and help her through the last couple of yards. They pushed him onto the riverbank and placed him on his side. Soon he started coughing, and water came out of his mouth. His breathing became regular, and his color improved within seconds. Colette breathed a sigh of relief. Robert would be fine. Her whole body ached, and she knew it would be a lot worse tomorrow, but she had managed to save that idiot's life. All in a good day's work, she thought as she smiled to herself.

Adam was observing her. He was extremely impressed with her coolness under pressure. She had not panicked. She had done exactly what needed to be done to save the young man without putting her life in danger. He was so proud of her. And at that very moment, he knew he wanted her to be his and his alone.

***

Adam had hired the talents of the hotel's concierge to find the perfect ring. Today was the day. They had gone to the Cluny Museum, and he was waiting for the right time to propose. Finally, in the medieval gardens, in the *jardin d'amour*, by those beautiful roses, Adam went on one knee and asked Colette to marry him. She did not reply right away. She looked stunned. Adam was holding his breath. He had never considered the option that she would turn him down. He had had to rush through the courtship because he was going home soon. He wanted her with him. He wanted her. And after what seemed like an eternity, Colette said a simple, barely audible yes.

Adam rose and kissed her hard. She was finally his. Colette did not pull back, but she was surprised that she was not seeing stars. She had always assumed that she would see them when she kissed her husband. But those were childish notions, she had told herself. She was now a grown woman about to get married to an intelligent, handsome, witty, and charming American professor.

CHAPTER 3

The next couple of weeks were a combination of joy and sorrow. Colette's family was showing a supportive united front, but her grandmother was spending more time than usual wiping her eyes. She had claimed her allergies were really bad this time of year. Pierre was telling jokes constantly, and Colette had even heard someone crying in the bathroom a few days earlier. She had to admit that she also had mixed feelings. On the one hand, she was marrying a man who would put most of her male friends to shame. He was so manly. On the other hand, she was going to move halfway around the world and rarely see her family, if she ever saw them again.

Adam had taken care of all the paperwork with the help of Colette's friend Anne. Everything was ready to go. Rather than have a church wedding, for which they did not have time, they would marry at city hall. The important thing was that she become his wife in time for the long journey back. They would travel by boat to New York and then, after visiting with his family for a few days, they would take the train to San Francisco.

***

When Colette's father had heard the news, he had almost collapsed. His little girl was going to move halfway around the world, far, far from where he could protect her. There was only one thing he could do, and this would require that all of his contacts work on his behalf quickly.

Time was of the essence. He took Colette aside and told her the family secret. She now needed to know.

So he started. "Honey, you are old enough to understand now. And as you are going away, I need to find a way to protect you even when I am not around. Your mother and I are Freemasons. We do not belong to the same Masonic body because we are of different genders, but we nonetheless have the same brothers and sisters."

Colette's mother interrupted. "You know, Colette, Freemasons are present all around the world. They keep their membership secret because of all the persecution they have suffered through history, and most recently in Spain, but they will always welcome and help a brother or sister in need."

Colette's father continued the explanation. "It normally takes a long time to gain membership, and the person who wants to join generally has to ask herself. But here we do not have time. I want you to trust me and become a Freemason before you leave. What do you say?"

Colette was taken aback by this revelation. She had had no idea. She knew of Freemasons and their moral values, and she even suspected that she had known some Masons. But her own parents? That was a surprise. She decided on the spot that if her membership would make her father feel better about her leaving, that was the least she could do.

So she agreed. And a few days later, she was initiated into her mother's lodge. Many rules had been broken, but her parents' influence had made this possible. She was made aware of the responsibilities that came with the membership and received a small list of women and men who lived in the United States and who would welcome her once she got there. No one was to know that they themselves were

Freemasons, and her own membership was to remain a secret. She was given the signs that would help her make contact, and she said good-bye to the women who had welcomed her into the sisterhood just a few hours prior.

***

To Colette's parents' dismay, the wedding was a quick event, and their daughter spent her wedding day busily closing up her suitcases rather than being the belle of the ball. In fact, just before the ceremony, Colette's dad had asked her, "Honey, is this really what you want to do? You are still so young, and you have so much time ahead of you. I am worried you were rushed into this and did not think it through."

Colette looked at her dad with a brave smile on her face and replied, "I really want to do this. Don't worry; I will be fine." And she walked to her seat to wait for the mayor to link her life to Adam's forever.

***

For the first time in her life, Colette woke up as Mrs. Adam Walker. Her wedding night had been even more surprising than her first kiss. Adam had come to bed, taken off her nightgown along with his own clothes, spread her legs, and plunged into her as if he was diving into the ocean. The initial pain had been so intense that it had taken her breath away. But after a minute or so, the whole process became something that might have been enjoyable if her husband had given her a little more time to warm up to the idea. "There has to be more to it than that," thought Colette as she waited for her husband to wake up.

Tired of looking at Adam's sleeping figure, Colette got up and went to the kitchen to take her last breakfast with her family. Grandmamma had been crying. It was obvious. So had her mother and sister, who were wearing sunglasses in the house. The mood was somber, and the breakfast just did not taste the same. It had a bittersweet quality that Colette knew she would never forget. And as she was walking back to her room to get dressed, her grandfather stopped her in the hallway. He reached into his pocket and pulled out his gold pen, the one he always wrote with, the one that had been with him since he had been a very young man.

He handed it to Colette and said, "Here, you take it with you. This way I know you will always have a pen to write with...and to remember me by."

He kissed her cheek and left without another word. Colette stood there committing to memory the smell of her grandfather's aftershave. He was such a gentle man, a man of few words. But he was always there to lend a sympathetic ear and offer advice when asked. Colette had known that it would break her heart to say good-bye to her family, but she had not realized how difficult it would really be. And two hours before her departure, she finally felt the overwhelming desperation that came with her decision.

Before she knew it, her travel trunks were in the car and she was standing on the sidewalk kissing everyone good-bye.

Her grandmother managed to hold the tears long enough to whisper in Colette's ear, "You are the firstborn of my grandchildren. There has always been a special bond between us, Colette. I will always love you the most. But this is our secret."

Then she kissed her granddaughter's cheek and walked back into the house.

The rest of the family kissed her in silence, too afraid that words would break the dam that prevented their tears from flowing freely. All the women were wearing sunglasses even though the sky was as gray as their mood. Even Anne, who had come for the occasion, was following this new trend.

She hugged her friend fiercely and said, "That pen your grandfather gave you is also good for writing to your friend. Don't forget me, and know that I will always be here for you if you need me."

And before Colette could reply, Adam pushed her in the car. And with a coldness that was new to their relationship, he told his wife, "Don't you think you have made enough of a spectacle of yourself?"

Colette's anger rose to the occasion. How could her new husband be so insensitive to her pain? How could he even make such a comment when she was doing all she could not to start sobbing like a little child? She had just abandoned her family, broken their hearts, and possibly made the biggest mistake of her life. And as she took one last look at them she saw a tear escape from behind her godmother's sunglasses. She wished she could wipe that tear away and make the older woman feel better, but she knew it would be a long time before she could kiss her cheeks and hug her again.

**

They traveled to Brest to catch the ship that would take them to America, and once onboard, things seemed to get a little better. Adam relaxed and slowly became his charming self again. Thankfully, neither Adam nor she seemed to be affected by sea sickness. Maybe Colette had overreacted. Adam was able to make her laugh almost constantly. Yes, she would be happy with him.

They spent their days walking on the deck and their nights making love. Even in that department, things had improved. The experience was enjoyable, and falling asleep in Adam's arms was very reassuring. He must love her. After all, he was always so physical, holding her hand, reaching for her when they crossed other couples on the deck, putting his arms around her shoulders when she looked cold during their evening stroll. He had even requested a table for two, where they took all their meals together, uninterrupted by the other passengers' discussions.

But sometimes he still had reactions that puzzled and worried her a little. One day, she had been writing a letter to her family to tell them about her wonderful cruise when Adam walked in.

After inquiring about her current activity, he grabbed the piece of paper she had been writing on, tore it into small pieces, and said, "I am your family now, darling. You really should concentrate on me."

Colette instinctively knew not to reply or even make eye contact. She got up from the desk and walked up to her husband. With a shy little smile, she went on tiptoe and kissed him on the mouth. Adam did not need any more encouragement than that to take his wife to bed, even in the middle of the afternoon.

Even though she was enjoying her husband's company, Colette could not wait to land on the American continent. She would meet her new brothers and sister, her mother-in-law, and hopefully the father-in-law Adam hardly ever talked about. She suspected the relationship between the two men was tense, but her husband had not shared any of the specifics with her.

***

Finally the big day arrived. They were taken to Ellis Island, where Colette was processed in a flash with her husband's help. She was shocked to see the long line of immigrants waiting for their fate to be decided while she was being ushered from one office to the next, each time getting closer to the exit point. Indeed, Adam had showed some paperwork and an official-looking card, and that seemed to have been enough to get them out of the immigration building rapidly. She had no idea what the card was. Every time she got close to seeing it, Adam would somehow find a way to obstruct her view. And before she knew it, she was out on the street, ready for her new adventure to begin.

As it was the end of July, New York was really hot and humid. Colette had never thought it possible for the weather to be as inclement as it was in Paris before a summer thunderstorm. But New York was by far the dampest and warmest environment she had ever experienced. And then she saw them. They all looked a little like Adam. They had the same golden hair and blue eyes, the same facial features, and the same broad shoulders. They were obviously all his brothers.

She had painstakingly learned all their names and distinguishing features while she was on the boat.

So she approached the first one and said, "You must be Joe. You are just as Adam described you. I am so pleased to meet you." And then she said to the next, "And you must be James." And she continued until she got to the last one. "You must be Peter, the youngest. You have the same name as my little brother. I just know we are going to get along famously," she said.

And the whole clan was in love with her instantly.

Adam was praised for his choice of bride. Even his father adored her. His sister could not have been happier to finally have a sibling of her own sex even if it was through marriage.

His mother took Colette everywhere. She introduced her to all her friends and even to some of her enemies. She seemed so proud of her new daughter-in-law. All were enthralled with Colette's personality, looks, homegrown sophistication, sweetness, and accent. She was the toast of the town.

***

One evening, as Colette was getting ready for one of the numerous parties she was attending, she heard a knock on the door. She opened it, and her mother-in-law walked in. She seemed in a hurry. The older woman grabbed her daughter-in-law's hands and kissed her soundly on the cheeks. Colette was stunned. With extreme rapidity, her mother-in-law had given her the recognition sign, and she was now smiling at her. Colette returned the coded signal and grinned right back. Her mother-in-law was also her sister. Her father had told her she would find Masons everywhere, but she was not expecting to meet one in her husband's family.

The older woman finally spoke. "Your mother's letter arrived today. So I was just informed. It did take some time for her to find me, but she did. And I am so glad. Adam knows nothing of my membership, and I think it would be wise if you did not divulge yours to him either."

The two women talked for a while longer and finally parted so Colette could finish getting ready.

Colette loved her new in-laws at least as much as they did her. She shared secrets with Stephanie, her sister-in-law, and the two young women went together to the symphony, to various stores, and even to the movie theater. And of course, a special bond had developed between Colette and her mother-in-law. Even the dreaded father-in-law had been a sweetheart. They had had a few conversations and had enjoyed reading the paper together every morning at breakfast. She could have stayed with her in-laws forever. But soon it was time to say good-bye again to go west and settle down in Berkeley, California, close to the university, where Adam taught Political Science.

CHAPTER 4

After their long train ride, they arrived in Oakland, California. The city was just a few miles from San Francisco, but it appeared to be a world away. As Colette exited the train station, she was shocked to see the poverty surrounding her. This was nothing like what she had read about in the various magazines her father had sometimes brought home for her mother. None of the glamour that had been described for her shone through here. This was not the California she was expecting. On top of that, Oakland was enjoying the advances of the nasty summer weather that San Francisco often experienced. Indeed, the weather was its usual summer day fog with temperature competing with a cold winter day in Paris. Colette had not expected this kind of climate at all. She had assumed that San Francisco was like the rest of California, which had been described to her by her teachers as being close to the French Riviera or even Morocco. And obviously this was neither. But in spite of that surprising turn of events, she welcomed the coolness that surrounded her after the tiring heat she had experienced day in, day out in New York.

She followed her husband to the taxicab that would take them home, and she prayed that her new place was far away from the destitute landscape she was now staring at. The houses were decrepit masses of peeling paint. Weather-beaten wooden shingles barely hung on the roofs, and children wearing rags were playing in water-filled potholes in front of their homes. The women were sitting on their front porches, disinterestedly watching their broods, probably wondering how they were going to feed them that night. Some held babies who appeared to be peacefully sleeping, unaware of the difficulties of life.

Colette felt instant relief when the cab left the area. And to her surprise, after a few minutes ride, the car stopped in front of a small yet quaint house. The street was quiet, and all the houses appeared well kept and nicely decorated. Obviously, this neighborhood had not been as touched by the Depression as the one she had seen by the station. Her husband took her hand and walked her to the white house with the beautiful rosebushes on each side of the door.

He opened the front door, and said, "Welcome home, honey. This place is now yours."

Colette looked around and decided that the residence needed a woman's touch. It was dark and stuffy. The interior was clean but lifeless. And soon she found out that Mrs. Pearce, the housekeeper, was responsible for the spotless environment Professor Walker was living in. Unfortunately, as kind as the old woman was, she did not have a taste for decoration, and thus that job had been left to Adam. And the result was as expected: functional, somewhat comfortable, but extremely ugly. As the woman of the house, Colette would have to change all that, and fast. Her sanity and well-being depended on it. She would have to get flowers from the garden. At least that would quickly add a touch of color to the austere décor. But that would have to wait.

Adam had taken her straight to the bedroom, where he had demonstrated the comfort of his home. They had both fallen asleep soon after, exhausted by the trip and the efforts they had just exerted.

Colette woke up feeling sticky and in need of a bathroom call. She got out of bed and started looking for the appropriate room. On the way, she found Adam's study with all the books he had accumulated and the papers he was working on lying here and there, sometimes on his big mahogany desk, sometimes on shelves, and even occasionally on the floor. This room was definitely not as clean as the rest of the house. Maybe Adam had declared it off limits to the poor woman in charge of maintaining order in his house. Or maybe he was just a very quick worker and could make a mess in his office as rapidly as he could have orgasms in bed.

***

The next few days were just spent going from one house to the next, meeting all of Adam's friends and colleagues. Colette felt like a monkey at the zoo. She was the object of so much scrutiny that she sometimes wanted to go home and hide in her room for the next few months. Besides, she was not sure she liked these people. They drank too much, were too loud, and sometimes too friendly. She had had to fight off the advances of the English department dean and the groping hands of Professor Henri Williams, Adam's best friend. But day after day, her husband insisted on going to these parties. And soon enough it was time to return all the invitations and host their own.

Colette could finally do something she enjoyed. She was going to make them all her favorite dishes and hoped that at last they would take the time to actually get to know her. So she asked Mrs. Pearce to show her where she could shop for the ingredients she needed. The older woman graciously obliged. Colette had liked Mrs. Pearce instantly. The old woman was a widow and had not been blessed with children. So she took her role as Colette's advisor very seriously.

Their first stop was at the butcher shop, and once again Colette was surprised. The meat was not prepared the same way as it was in France. She could not recognize any of the cuts she was used to. So she spent some time discussing her dinner plans with the very knowledgeable butcher's wife to determine what her best options were for her planned dinner. By the time she left the store, she was relieved to have met this wonderful woman who was so eager to help, and she was happy with the purchases she had just made.

Their second stop was at the small grocery store just a block from her house. Mrs. Pearce introduced her to the owner's wife, Rosie. The young woman had a friendly smile and a strong, honest handshake. She looked people straight in the eyes, while her own eyes reflected all the kindness and decency she carried inside. Colette liked her instantly. She made her purchases and promised to come back very soon for a longer chat. Rosie was the first person who seemed to really care about Colette's thoughts and opinions. She had not undressed her with her eyes, nor had she asked her where she had bought her clothes or how much she had paid for them. And that was greatly appreciated.

The third stop was at the bakery. Yet again, Colette was in for a shock. There was no French bread, no baguette, no *pain de campagne*, only some strange-looking dinner rolls and a mushy loaf of bread. The dessert, she realized, would have to be homemade because there was no decent fruit tart around.

So she rushed home and started cooking frantically. Dinner was ready to serve on time, the dessert was cooling in the pantry, and Colette had even had time for a quick bath and a change of clothes before all the guests arrived. Mrs. Pearce could set the table before she went home, and Adam could entertain his friends for a few minutes alone if Colette needed extra time to get ready. She wanted to look beautiful for her husband and make him proud.

And proud Adam was. The dinner was a success. Colette was a fine cook, and French cuisine was already considered one of the best in the world. The guests were enthused by the meal, the setting, and the hostess. One of them even commented,

"Those little pastries are just like little bites of heaven." Colette held her tongue as she watched the woman scarf down most of the platter, but she thought, "Watch it, lady, soon these little bites of heaven are going to be hell on your hips."

Yes, the hostess of the day had pulled it off. She looked magnificent in her semiformal cocktail dress, and for once she actually had some intelligent conversation regarding world events and the slow recovery from the economic fiasco the United States and Europe had experienced.

When the guests finally left, Adam retired to his study while Colette tidied up the living and dining room. She was taking the garbage out in the dark when she hit what felt like a brick wall, nearly knocking her off her feet. Fortunately, the brick wall had strong arms and hands that steadied her before she preceded the refuse into the trash can.

"I'm so sorry," the wall said," I was not expecting anyone here at this time of night. My name is John. I'm your next-door neighbor and a student at the university. Well, actually, I will be starting next week."

Colette looked up and saw that her talking wall was none other than a young Asian man about her own age.

And with a big smile on her face, she replied, "My name is Colette. I am Professor Walker's wife. It is very nice to meet you, John. If you will forgive me, I will extricate myself from this rather smelly situation. But I would love to continue our conversation in full daylight and by the rosebushes, if it can be helped. I am sure it would be much more agreeable to both of us."

John laughed at her introduction and promised to take her up on her offer as he watched her retreat into the darkness.

CHAPTER 5

Colette had been married to Adam for two months when she realized she had not had a period since before the wedding. She wished Mrs. Pearce was still around so she could ask her for advice, but the old woman had retired and moved in with her sister, who lived in Sacramento. She had felt that now that the professor was married, he did not need her services anymore. So Colette went to see Rosie to ask her for the name and address of a local doctor. Rosie obliged and even took Colette to him herself. The two women had become friends very quickly. And both were overjoyed to learn that Colette was pregnant. Her baby was to be born the following April.

The expectant mother could not wait to give her husband the good news, so she decided to visit him at his office on the university campus. It took her some time to locate the appropriate building and even longer to find the right office. The door was slightly open, which allowed her to see that there was a beautiful blonde sitting on her husband's desk. He was apparently discussing the finer points of his prior lecture. The woman was most likely a student, and Colette was appalled at how this girl was throwing herself at her husband. Expectant mother or not, Colette really wanted to teach her a lesson, scratch her eyes out and pull all her hair so she would look like the hairless rat she was. But instead, she took a deep breath and walked right in.

She went to her husband, kissed him right on the mouth, and said, "Hello, darling." She then turned to the student, and with a big smile told her, "Hello, I'm Mrs. Walker, Professor Walker's wife. You must be one of his students."

The blonde looked shocked and a little embarrassed. She got up, mumbled some good-byes, and left as quickly as she could.

Satisfied that she had erased the competition without causing an embarrassing scene, Colette turned to her bewildered husband and said, "I came here because I could not wait to give you the good news. I went to see the doctor this morning, and we are going to have a baby."

The professor went from bewildered to stunned in half a second flat. He could not believe his ears. He was going to have to share his wife with a baby. He had always known this would eventually happen, but he had hoped it would take a lot longer. Besides, he had never thought that his governmental activities went well with having children. This was just not going according to plan. The wife asset was turning into a liability, and fast. He did not speak.

Colette was surprised. She had expected a joyous response, one that would show her how much her husband wanted the baby. After all, he had told her that his mom was pressuring him to get married and have a child.

Finally, he looked at her and said, "We'll talk about it tonight when I get home. I have a lecture to give in five minutes."

***

Colette had been waiting for hours. Dinner was cold. The living room was dark, and still there was no sign of Adam. When midnight struck, she went to bed. She was crying silently when she finally heard the front door. She stayed put and waited for him to join her. He finally walked in the room. He smelled of alcohol and tobacco. He was not very steady on his legs and almost fell on her when he went to grab her. He ripped her nightgown, turned her over, and without a single word, took her with a roughness she had never experienced before. He then rolled over and went to sleep. Colette felt humiliated. He had taken her like an animal, had given her no respect, and she did not even understand why.

She had wanted to talk to him, to try to understand where all this anger and hatred had come from. But when she woke up, he was gone. And it was just as well. A wave of nausea went through her, and she had to sprint to the bathroom to make it to the toilet on time. Things could not get any worse. Her husband hated her, and her baby made her so sick she could hardly move. If only Rosie could come and walk her through this.

As if her friend had sensed her need, the doorbell rang. And when Colette opened the door, Rosie was standing right there with a questioning look. She said, "I came by because I got worried when you did not stop by this morning at your usual time. What's going on?" She grabbed Colette with both arms and wrapped her in a blanket that was thrown negligently on the sofa. As Colette told her friend what had happened, Rosie became incensed. What was Adam thinking? Had he gone completely mad? On top of the humiliation he had inflicted on his wife, he could have hurt the baby. Rosie's husband would give anything to have a child. They had been trying for six long years, and nothing. The doctor had even suggested they adopt. But they kept on trying. And as difficult as it would be to see Colette's pregnancy develop, Rosie would be by her side to support her. That's what friends did. They helped each other.

The women spent the day together after Rosie told her husband what happened. The poor man had shaken his head and told them to let him know if they needed any help.

As they walked back toward Colette's house, they ran into John, who was coming back from class.

"Hello, John. It's so nice to see you again, and this time in a setting that must be so much more pleasant on your nose. At least you will now know for sure that I was not trying on a new French perfume," she said, laughing.

John laughed also, turned different shades of red, and finally whispered, "I never thought that for a minute."

He said his good-byes and ran home.

Rosie, who had not missed a beat, inquired as to what was going on. Colette explained how they had met and that John was just the next-door neighbor who was attending the university.

Rosie frowned and asked, "Are you aware that John really likes you?"

"John does not know me," Colette replied. "Besides, he knows I am married."

That was really irrelevant, and both girls knew that.

And before Rosie went home, Colette decided it was time to tell her friend about her Masonic lineage. She would need her help in contacting some of the women on the list her parents had given her.

Upon hearing the confession, Rosie smiled and just said, "I had the feeling you were one of us."

She proceeded to give Colette the sign, and when the young woman returned it, she said, "We are sisters. I should have known. Our next lodge meeting is next week. I will take you to the meeting and introduce you to the others."

***

In the next few months, Colette often crossed paths with John. The young man seemed to always be coming back from school or leaving for an errand when Colette was coming home with grocery bags. He would help her bring them in and put things away. He would then respectfully say good-bye and disappear until the next time she brought groceries home.

Every morning she could see him do a series of strange moves in his backyard. He was oblivious to the fact that she could see him as he was practicing what appeared to be a form of martial arts. He always practiced bare chested, wearing only loose black pants that moved with his limber legs. Hiding behind her curtains, Colette could see the ripples of perfectly shaped muscles as he performed the exercises. He was a beautiful man with an equally beautiful body. But she was married.

So to alleviate her conscience, when she would discuss her morning show with Rosie, she would tell her friend, "Yes, I know. I am married. But really, it does not matter where I get my appetite as long as I eat at home. And I assure you that I only eat at home."

Her friend would laugh at the French woman's outrageousness.

Colette was starting to show, and John and she had talked about her pregnancy once. But he was always very discreet and never asked any questions that might embarrass her. But one day, as they were putting the groceries away, the baby kicked for the first time. Colette stopped and put her hand to her baby bump. John got scared and asked, "Are you okay?" Colette did not reply but grabbed his hand and placed it on her abdomen as well. The baby kicked again, and this time into John's hand, as if to say hello to his mother's friend. The young man was in shock. He had just felt a baby moving inside a woman for the first time in his life. And this baby should have been his. He would have been such as good husband to Colette. He had loved her from afar for months, and was smart enough to know that he would never have her. However, he would always be there for her.

***

With the support of her friends, Colette's pregnancy was moving along just fine. After Rosie had taken her to the lodge meeting to meet her sisters and start her formal training as a Mason, she had had a complete support network that made her life much easier. Sure, she was not good friends with all of them, but they had all demonstrated over time that they would all be there for her if she needed help. And at this point, that was all that mattered. She had heard from her parents through her sisters at the lodge and preferred to keep it that way so Adam would not be annoyed with her.

***

Ever since Adam had found out that Colette was pregnant, he had been just horrible. But Colette wanted to make things right. She would have the baby soon, and she wanted Adam to love this child as much as she did. So she decided to take his lunch to him so they could eat together at his desk. But when she got to his office, what she found on his desk was not lunch…well, at least not hers. Indeed, Adam was busy having sex with yet another student of his. That explained a lot. Now she knew why the big professor had not touched her in almost three months, why he was so uninvolved with his child's arrival, and why her pregnancy had been such an ordeal. Thank God there was John…and Rosie…and all the other women…of course.

The walk back to her house was one of the most painful she had ever taken. The humiliation she had suffered that night months earlier was nothing compared to the one she had just suffered. He had known she had been there, yet he had opted not to stop. She had stared at him unable to move for a few minutes. She could not catch her breath. Her chest was swelling almost as quickly as her ankles. At that point she knew deep in her heart she would never forgive him. She ran out of the building eager to hide from her husband, the humiliation, and the pain She started to cry. She was crying for the loss of an ideal she realized she would never have. She was crying because her child would never know what it was like to have parents who loved and respected each other. She was crying because she should have paid more attention to her father's warning. He had been right. She barely knew Adam. In fact, she did not know him at all.

Then the pain of the contractions started. She stumbled up the few steps that took her to her front door and collapsed. The pain was so intense, and her tears blinded her. Her water broke. She was going to have that baby on her front lawn. The neighbors would be very displeased with such an inappropriate scene, and so would her husband. But as usual when she needed him, John ran to her. From the window just in front of his desk, he had seen her fall. He cradled her head and calmed her down. He needed to understand what was going on if he was to help her.

He said, "You are going to have your baby. Where is your husband? I will go get him."

She started crying again and begged him not to go. As he was about to send one of his roommates, she told him the whole story. John almost vomited. He wanted to kill Adam. He wanted to hurt him first and then kill him. How could he even consider hurting such a beautiful, kind, and gentle woman?

But soon the young man said, "Okay. I will send for the doctor, and I will take you inside."

After summoning his friend, he took Colette in his arms and carried her all the way up the stairs to her bedroom. He put her on her bed and told her to relax as much as possible until the doctor arrived. But Colette would not let him go. She was holding on to his hand as if it were her only way out of this nightmare. So he stayed. He stroked her hair and held her hand with the other. And he felt and lived through every one of her agonizing contractions. He wanted to stop the pain, make her better, and give her a rest. But he knew she had to go through this alone.

The doctor finally arrived, and John was pushed out of the room. Colette's eyes were huge as she watched her friend leave the room. He knew she wanted him to stay, but he also knew that her wish, for once, could not be his command. He would wait right by the door until it was over or until her husband came home.

He heard her scream and the doctor direct. She was losing steam. He could feel it. And then it dawned on him that she could die. His beloved Colette could leave this earth and never know how he truly felt about her. He could not let that happen. He tried to walk in, but the door was locked. He guessed the doctor had had more than a few dads come in and try to help when they should have been outside. And the screaming stopped. And John's heart almost stopped along with it. Until he heard a tiny little scream. Someone in that room was not pleased with the doctor right now.

And to his great relief, he heard her laugh, and the doctor said, "You have a son, my dear, a beautiful, healthy baby boy."

And overwhelmed with relief, John started to cry. She had survived. The love of his life would not go away today. After what seemed like an eternity, the door opened, and he was allowed in. Colette looked so tired yet so happy with her baby resting in her arms.

She smiled at him and told him, "John, come meet George. I do believe he has wanted to shake your hand for some time."

John approached the newborn baby and took the tiny hand in his. The baby stirred and looked at him with his brand-new eyes.

The young man was about to speak when Adam walked in, furious and belligerent.

"Get out, you stupid kid. I can take care of my own family!" blurted the professor.

Colette did not want John to go, ever. But she could not find a good reason for him to stay. After all, Adam was the baby's father and her husband.

However, she came to John's defense and told her husband, "You should be thanking him, Adam, instead of insulting him. While you were dishonoring your marriage vows on your desk with your student, this man was kind enough to help me into the house and get the doctor to deliver your son. I will thank you to be courteous to him because had he not been there, the neighbors would have feasted their eyes on your child's birth and his mother's less than elegant position to accommodate the dear child's will. I will never forgive you."

John said his good-byes to Colette and left. The little, frail, gentle woman could say it like it was. And she had let her husband bear the shame with her. She had been humiliated, but she was not going to hide. Good for her!

CHAPTER 6

Adam had been a very attentive husband and father in the last few months. He was really trying to make it up to Colette. Unfortunately, his efforts had come a little too late. She would never forget. She would stay with him for her son's sake. She would be a good wife, but she would be a better mother. And she had told him so. This child was hers and hers alone. She still performed her wifely duties and even pretended to enjoy it. She made the home comfortable for everyone and made sure George had all the attention he needed. He was a beautiful baby, with the dark hair he had inherited from his mother and the blue eyes from his father.

As a matter of fact, he looked a lot like Adam. But even this resemblance was not enough to keep the father interested for long. And soon enough, Adam was back to his old tricks. Coming home late or not at all was a common occurrence. And Colette was raising the baby on her own. Adam had also started traveling east on a regular basis. And this was not helping one bit.

John and Rosie would come and visit often. They would play with the baby and allow Colette a few minutes of adult conversation and relaxation time. But one day, Adam came home with a few drinks under his belt while her friends were visiting. As he walked in the room, he looked at John and roared, "Colette, I do not want this kid in my home."

Ever so sweetly, Colette replied, "My dear Adam, you lost your right to tell me what I can and cannot do, whom I can or cannot see, the day you threw your student on your desk and had sex with her. This kid, as you call him, is more of a man than you will ever be. At least he was here when my son was born. You, on the other hand, were probably out drinking or worse. So I would appreciate it very much if you remained civil to my friends." And Adam stormed out without another word. He would not even tell her he was leaving for Washington, DC, soon. She would find out anyway. But not from him...

***

It was about midnight, and Adam had not come home. George was getting fussier by the minute, and he seemed to get hotter as well. He had had three bright-green bowel movements in the last hour and was not doing well. So Colette walked to the doctor's house with the baby in her arms to have him look at the little one. And as soon as she got there, the man took the baby from her and started palpating and listening.

He finally turned to Colette, and with a little voice she had never heard before, he said, "George has probably caught the bug that is going around. Unfortunately there is absolutely nothing I can do. Try and keep him hydrated. If he survives the night, he should be okay. But the odds are not good. A few people in the county have already lost their children to this disease. I will stop by in the morning to see how you are doing."

Colette felt as if she had been hit right in the solar plexus. She could not breathe or talk. She could barely walk. She took the baby and left.

As she was managing one step after another, she decided that she would fight for her baby's life with all her might. She would go to John and ask for his help yet again. And Rosie. Rosie could help too.

She knew her friends would not let her down, would not let George down.

And so, in the middle of the night, she knocked on John's door. When he opened, she briefly explained what was going on. Of course Adam was nowhere to be found.

So John took over and said, "I am going to get my friend's car, and I will drive you to Chinatown. There is a Chinese doctor there who can help your baby." And having said that, he disappeared.

**

The smell of the herbs was overwhelming. Colette had never seen so many of them. She walked to the back of the store where John was already talking to an old Chinese man. The doctor took George and started feeling the baby's pulse, looking at his hands, probing his belly, feeling the baby's forehead, and smelling the diaper. He then took a needle out and poked George's ear right at the top. The baby screamed, but the little Chinese man kept working and making the ear bleed. Soon he touched the baby's forehead again and looked satisfied.

He said, "Good. Baby's fever down. Now we stop diarrhea."

He took more needles out and started poking the baby here and there with the efficiency of someone who had a lifetime of experience. He worked feverishly for a few minutes and stopped again. He then turned the baby around and started pulling at the skin of the child's back right on the spine.

He then looked at Colette and said, "You do this every day. It will help baby fight diseases. I give you herbs. You give baby every day too, for three days. Baby will be fine."

He then went behind the counter where all the herbs were and started putting together a formula specific to George's condition. He explained to Colette how she should cook the herbs and then walked John, Colette, and George to the door.

***

George had quieted down, and the diarrhea seemed to have stopped for now. The car ride was helping him sleep, and Colette could barely keep her eyes open. For the first time in a long time, she could finally relax. She fell asleep, and her head came to rest on John's shoulder. So when they arrived home, he dared not wake her. He sat there looking at mother and child until the sun came up and they both stirred. Colette smiled at John and thanked him profusely.

She would never forget that he had saved her son's life.

Now that George was out of danger, she invited John over for coffee. She wanted to discuss what they had lived through the previous night, and she wanted to know more about the medicine that the Chinese doctor had performed on her baby.

John obliged and started explaining. "The man you saw practices Chinese medicine, which includes acupuncture, bleeding when necessary, herbs, tui na (a form of massage), cupping, moxibustion, and a few other modalities. This medicine is thousands of years old, and millions of people use it as their main source of healing. It takes years of training to become a good practitioner. And Doctor Chang has been doing it for years. He is my family's physician and has been treating me since I was born. In fact, most Chinese people in San Francisco go to their own Chinese practitioner instead of a white doctor. They cook their herbs every day and drink their tea like we do water. The interesting part is that, in ancient times, the Chinese doctor was paid regularly to keep people from getting sick. But when they got sick, he would treat them for free. The idea was that if they got sick, it was because the doctor had not done his job properly and thus their body had not been kept in balance. It was therefore the doctor's duty to care for them free of charge."

Colette was fascinated.

She asked, "How can I learn this medicine? I want George to benefit from it, but Doctor Chang lives so far away."

"I will see what I can do. I am going to visit my parents this weekend. I will go talk to Master Chang while I am in the city. Who knows, he may be willing to teach you," John replied.

**

As promised, John stopped by Master Chang's clinic and asked the old man if he would take on Colette as a student.

"I no teach women! But she can come sweep floor," the Chinese man replied. "I will see her every weekend."

The old man had sensed something in Colette. This woman was unusual. She had a gift, and he knew it. But the rules were the rules. First, potential students must not only demonstrate their interest but also their will to endure and be taught in sometimes unorthodox ways. And they had to have patience. Lots of patience. So Master Chang would see if he was right about her. But he did not share any of this with the young man who had come with her request.

John went back to Colette and reported his conversation.

He expected her to be distraught, but instead, the young woman smiled and announced, "I will do it. You know…he will teach me. I know it."

**

A week later, Colette started her "formal" education with Doctor Chang. It had been decided that every time John would go to visit his parents, he would take Colette and the baby to the old Chinese man who would let her sweep the floor until John picked her up again that night. Mrs. Chang would watch the baby.

Doctor Chang would see patients all day with an apprentice by his side. The old man would take the patient's pulse, take a look at the tongue, ask a few questions, diagnose, insert needles, and write an herbal formula that his shadow apprentice would prepare for him.

Colette would always manage to be sweeping near the master when he was diagnosing. She would then ask the apprentice to repeat to her in English what the teacher had said in Chinese. And within a few months, Colette could accurately predict some of the simpler cases.

Her skill grew so that one day she saw the tongue of a patient and mumbled, "Heat condition. Probably yin deficiency."

The old Chinese man turned to her and asked, "What did you say?"

Colette repeated what she had just said, embarrassed by the fact that she had spoken out loud when she thought she was only thinking the words.

The old man then asked, "How do you know?"

Colette explained, "Well, the tongue is red, which indicates heat in the body. And then there is no coat, which points to a yin deficiency."

Then the master asked, "Anything else you can tell me?"

So Colette continued, "I think there may be some spleen deficiency as well because the sides of the tongue are scalloped. But I am not sure."

"Not bad. Do you know what to do now?" the master asked.

"I'm afraid not, Doctor Chang. After all, I just sweep the floors," Colette replied.

The old man laughed and said, "Okay. I will teach you. Be ready next weekend."

From that point on, Colette would come home with herb samples to study, as well as acupuncture charts and tons of notes she had taken during the day. George would stay with the doctor's wife, who enjoyed having a little one around to take care of. The old woman would also share recipes with Colette, as Chinese medicine is as much a healing art as it is a way of life. And the young woman learned how to use the herbs she was studying as spices in her food.

She learned about the culture too. One day, she asked the old doctor a question.

He looked at her and said, "You ask too many questions. You would make a bad wife and daughter-in-law. But you make a good doctor."

Colette was surprised by what she had just heard. She took advantage of her friendship with Mrs. Chang and asked more questions about the proper behavior of a Chinese wife. At the same time, she found out that, like white people, the Chinese also wanted to marry within their own race. They wanted their children to be Chinese so they could be immersed in their culture as well. In many ways what they wanted of their life was no different from your typical Anglo-American family. The only difference was the submission that was expected of wives and daughters-in-law. Dr. Chang was right. She would definitely be a bad one.

The more Colette learned, the more she wanted to know. As a matter of fact, Master Chang had never met such a quick study. She was zooming through the material and would soon be able to treat simple cases on her own. She had started helping him around the clinic soon after she started her formal training with him, and she was a natural. She did not use the standard Chinese way of activating the acupuncture point energies, which entailed either moving the needle up and down into the skin or rolling it back and forth until the body grabbed the needle and held on to it. Instead, it seemed to the old man that the activation came from her own fingers, as if she was transferring some of her own energy to establish the connection between the needles and the patient she was treating. The clients loved her style because it did not hurt. And really, who liked pain? Besides, he did not know of any Chinese doctors where she lived, and he knew from experience that the white man's medicine could not do it all. A Chinese medicine presence near the university would be a welcome addition. Just a few more months…

***

Adam had been disappearing more often and for longer periods of time. He would not tell Colette where he was going, and she would not ask. It was obvious that he had another life somewhere, where she was not allowed to go, and she had long ago decided that she was okay with that. For now.

CHAPTER 7

The war had broken out in Europe months ago. And even though the United States had declared their neutrality, it was obvious to Colette that they would eventually have to go to war as well. And the sooner the better, if Europe was going to survive. She had not heard from her family since the war had started, and she prayed every day that they all had survived the German attacks and occupation. France had capitulated just a few months after the onset of the conflict, but as far as the rumors went, French citizens were organizing a resistance all over the nation. Unfortunately, she knew what war could do to a country. She had been born only two years after the great one, as World War I was commonly referred to, and she had been raised on the stories of the horrors of the time. After all, her own father had fought in that one and had barely made it out alive. She had heard of the young men dying in the trenches, the hunger in the streets, and the homeless orphans left to their own demise.

The necessity for the involvement of the United States in the conflict was one subject Adam and she agreed on. As a matter of fact, he had shared with her that he was spending more and more time in Washington, DC. He had been asked to advise on the appropriate development and war contingencies that the United States should implement. He might have been a sad imitation of a father and husband, but he was an expert in his field.

Colette decided that since Europe was at war and the United States would soon be, she would convert her whole yard at the back of the house into a vegetable and fruit garden. She told her friend Rosie to do the same and encouraged the whole neighborhood to join them. She had been told of the lack of food during the Great War and did not wish her friend and family to suffer as others in Europe had. She offered her expertise to anyone who wanted her help. As she had watched her father grow his small but very efficient vegetable garden for years, she knew what needed to be done. She organized hers so that potatoes would cover only one quarter of the planting area. She would rotate to another quarter the following year, and so on. The rest of the garden was used for tomatoes, green beans, carrots, bell peppers, strawberries, and melons. She also had an orange and an apple tree.

She trained her sisters in the art of gardening and then enrolled their help in training others. She taught them how to teach and sent them to their own neighborhoods to start their own programs. The more people who were involved, the less hunger would be seen.

She had started her own garden in the spring of '39 a few weeks before George was born. She had learned to can what her family could not eat during the summer months, so she had vegetables year round. She had taught Rosie and the others the following year, so her friends and neighbors would be ready when the time came. And Colette knew it was only a matter of time before things got really tough.

She had also shared her fears with John, who had decided to teach her how to drive. He knew that if Colette was right, he would not be there to take her to Dr. Chang's, or wherever she needed to go. She needed to be independent so she could survive on her own. So twice a week, he took her driving. The first time was probably the only time he actually feared for his life. The woman had almost put the car in a ditch and had not even realized what was happening because she was talking. Had it been anyone other than Colette, John would have walked away and never looked back. But it was she. And so he got his temper in check and then suggested she concentrate on the road and stop talking, if she could. After all, she was a woman. She might not be able to, John thought. And he was relieved to see in the next few weeks that at least this one woman had the ability to be quiet and pay attention. He was thrilled. Within a month, Colette was proficient at driving, and John felt confident that she could do it on her own.

And on December 7, 1941, Colette's world changed forever. Late that night, two men in army uniforms knocked at the door and asked to speak to Adam. The professor took them to his study for a private conversation. When he came out, he looked very somber. He waited for his guests to leave and then told Colette he had been called to serve his country, in an official capacity this time. He would have to be in Washington full-time until further notice. He might then be sent elsewhere, but for now he would be on American soil. He would be safe. After months of leading a double life, he finally explained to Colette that he was an intelligence gatherer and an analyst for the president of the United States. His disappearances had been linked to his work with the government. He should have told her. But he had been mad at her and had wanted to get back at her. Now, though, with the war a reality, he wanted her to know the truth.

The very next day, Colette said good-bye to Adam, not knowing when he was going to come back. Things were going to change drastically in the next few months. Colette would have to find a job soon, because her savings would quickly run out and Adam had not mentioned sending her any money. She would have to make do on her own.

When she discussed her predicament with Rosie, her friend suggested that she work for them at the store part-time and that she start practicing her healing arts the rest of the time. After all, more and more people were asking for her services. It was time that she started making a little money doing it. She would still continue her education with Master Chang and discuss her more difficult cases with him, but she could easily treat bronchitis, ear infections, and colds, not to mention Mrs. Pots's arthritis and Mr. Wayne's gout.

So she took Rosie up on her offer, and a little space in the store was set up with some of the most basic herbs Colette needed for her craft. She did not have all the nice wooden drawers that Doctor Chang had in his clinic, but the tin boxes she had labeled with a black marker would do nicely for now. She had arranged to have a chair in a corner where she could do most of her acupuncture treatments. She had also put together a travel kit that would allow her to do house calls as well. Rosie would watch George when she was gone. He was such an easy child. And little by little, she was getting excited about the idea of becoming a healer.

She was busy daydreaming when she heard the door of the store open. John walked in slowly, his face pale and his hands folding and unfolding a piece of paper nervously. He stood in front of Colette, who was looking at him, questions in her eyes. And after what appeared like an eternity, he finally said, "I ship out in one week. I am being sent to Hawaii." Colette almost fainted. She was as white as a fresh mozzarella slice and could not utter a word. She was sure her heart had stopped beating. She could not breathe. She could not lose John. Not now, not ever. And even though she was married to Adam and would remain so for the rest of her life, she knew then that John was and would always be the love of her life.

***

John and Colette spent as much time as they could together before the dreaded day arrived. Rosie had offered to watch George so the adults could have some time to say good-bye. The child would sleep at

Rosie's, and Colette could take the time she needed to grieve the loss of her friend.

So the young couple went out to dinner. Neither of them knew what they ate or how it tasted. And neither of them cared. They made small talk and avoided talking about the future. And then it was time to go home. They walked alongside each other, and John took Colette's hand in his. The fire that burned inside them was so intense they could not even speak anymore. And when they finally arrived at Colette's house, John put his hands on Colette's shoulders and forced her to face him.

With desperation in his voice, he said, "This is it. This is good-bye. I am leaving in a few hours, and there is something I want you to know."

Colette tried to stop him. Her eyes were filling with tears, and she did not know if she could take the heartbreak.

"Please let me finish. Otherwise, I may not have the courage to say what I have to say. Colette, I know I can never have you. But I love you nonetheless. I have loved you from the moment I bumped into you, and I will love you until I die. Sometimes it kills me to think of you with him. He does not deserve you. But you are married to him, and I respect that. Anyhow, I did not want to die without you knowing how I felt about you."

"Oh, John, you cannot die. I love you too much to lose you like that. You have to come back to me, so our friendship can go on, so I can see your children grow up with you at their side. I will never be their mother, and that is a fact I have to accept, but I can be their friend. I can be your friend. I love you now, and I always will." Colette blurted out with tears rolling down her face.

John was in shock. He had no idea she felt the same way. And suddenly he grabbed her face with both hands and started kissing her lips. She threw her arms around his neck and kissed him right back. What had been intended to be a gentle kiss good-bye quickly turned into an all-consuming, desperate, passionate embrace that shook them to the core. Their bodies were on fire. With a simple kiss, they were sharing themselves, their minds, their very souls. The world around them no longer existed. They were one.

And through a fog of need and want, John found the strength to finally stop kissing her. He was trembling from head to toe. He held her in his arms and embraced her with such strength she thought her bones would break right alongside her heart. And with an inner strength he did not know he possessed, he let her go and walked away. He felt her collapse on the porch and sob like he had never heard any human being cry. It took all his willpower to not turn back and comfort her. But he knew it would be even harder if he did. So he went home, and from his desk he watched her until dawn, knowing that she was dying inside. That night he decided that he would survive this war for her. No matter what.

***

Colette finally walked inside her house at dawn. She had cried for hours, and she was not feeling any better. She was numb inside and wondered how she would survive a lifetime without John. But first things first. He needed to come back alive from this stupid war. Then she could worry about the pain it would cause her to watch him marry another woman and have children with her. So for now she would pray every day for his safe return.

Having devised a plan of action, she decided to go to Rosie's to get her son. Being with George always made her feel better. Just the idea of seeing his lovely face and charming smile made her grin in return. She loved him more than anything. But when she arrived at the store, she saw that her friend had been crying as well.

Rosie looked at her and said, "Mike has been drafted. My husband will be leaving in three days. He has known for a few days already, but he did not know how to tell me. Isn't that grand?"

Colette took her friend in her arms and said, "I am so sorry, Rosie. I know I cannot replace Mike, but I will help you in the store as much as I can."

Soon a routine was established. Colette would arrive at the store early in the morning with George at her side. The women would have a cup of coffee and would share the news they had had from their warriors. Mike and John wrote every day, even if the letters sometimes arrived in packs of nine or ten. And sometimes there would be no news for weeks. Adam wrote about once a month, generally to give orders as to what Colette should be doing with her time.

But Colette was doing just fine without her husband. Her practice was flourishing, and the old doctor was finally warming up to the "new" kind of medicine Colette was practicing. She saw patients every day and kept very busy. She also helped Rosie with the store's supply delivery and with the ration coins she had to handle. As a merchant, not only did she have her personal ones to manage, but she also had to help others with the process. At night she would have dinner with Rosie and play with George until bedtime. She would then write John and occasionally Adam. She would finally go to bed herself and wake up the next day to start over.

But this morning things were different. She arrived at the store, only to see her friend with a piece of paper in her hands and tears streaking her cheeks. Rosie handed her the paper without a word.

"We regret to inform you that Michael Stern has died on January 3rd, 1943, while combating the enemy in the South Pacific. We extend our sincere condolences to his surviving family."

It was just a cold piece of paper, with a cold message, from a cold army. Rosie's husband was dead. She felt very sorry for her friend, but a little selfish part of her thanked God it was not John.

She turned her attention to her friend, who finally spoke. "Did you know that Mike and I could never have children? He died and left me nothing. I have no child of his to comfort me. I have no reason for living."

Colette could only let her talk and hold her. She knew full well how she would feel if anything ever happened to John, and she would not be hypocritical enough tell her friend that things would get better. She honestly did not know that they could—and certainly not if Rosie had loved Mike as much as she loved John.

But what Colette offered next surprised them both.

"Why don't we move in with you? George loves you as if you were his second mom. The restrictions are making it very difficult to keep two houses, and since we both work from the store, it would be easier to live here. However, if you prefer to move in with George and me, it can as easily be arranged," Colette blurted out.

And after a moment, Rosie replied, "You are right. I have the room here. We can still use your garden for harvest purposes, but we can save resources if you guys move in here. Let's do it."

Colette was relieved. Being with Rosie at this time was particularly important, and she knew that having George around always brought a smile to her friend's face.

Injured men had started coming home from the war. Some would visit Colette's tiny clinic in an attempt to alleviate their pain. And soon the young healer realized that the pain each man felt was as much in his head as it was in his body. And so she started treating both. And before she knew what was going on, she would have groups of them come and sit with needles in their ears. Some would talk about their experiences, while others would just sit and listen. And every day, they came back. They seemed to feel better.

A man named Harold was one of the regulars who came every morning. He walked with a cane because his left knee had been injured. Most days the pain was tolerable he had said. But the nights were full of trauma. He would relive the time he had spent in combat over and over again. He sometimes stayed after the treatment and talked with Rosie for some time. They seemed to be enjoying each other's company. Occasionally, he would ask Rosie out to dinner, and she would decline. But one day, to Colette's surprise, she said yes. Rosie had survived. She would be fine. She was coming back to the world of the living. It had been well over a year since Mike's passing.

Colette was happy for her friend. She wanted her to start enjoying life again. She, on the other hand, had put her own life on hold. Adam had been sent to Europe a few months back, and she had not heard from him since. Even John's letters were becoming scarcer. She had heard from some of the men that the fighting had yet again intensified. She was afraid. They were saying that the Allies were considering liberating Europe by landing on the coast of Normandy. This was pure madness. So many would die.

CHAPTER 8

Colette had just finished treating her last patient and was about to close the store for the night when a young woman walked in with her baby. She handed the bundle to Colette and said, "I just came from the doctor's office. My baby is burning up, and he has green diarrhea. The doctor told me to come and see you right away." Colette flashed back on that night when John had first taken her to see Master Chang. She knew she could help this baby. She went to get her needles, but they were all dirty. She called Rosie to the rescue and explained to her friend how she was to sterilize the needles. She then went back to the baby and instinctively put her hands on the little abdomen.

She felt a tingling sensation in her palms, and her hands were burning up. The baby fell asleep. She then pricked the little ears with a lancet to bleed them and watched the temperature go down within minutes. She put her hands on the baby again. She could hear that the growling was calming down. The movement in the intestines was slowing down. The baby was healing under her hands. She asked Rosie to prepare the formula as she was finishing working on the child. And after a good hour of tireless work, and no green bowel movement, Colette was able to return the resting bundle to his mom.

It was only when she walked the woman back to the door that she noticed two men in uniform standing in a corner of the store. They had waited for her to finish with her patient, but they now handed her a telegram from Adam. It said, "Brother in Resistance. Taken by Gestapo. Need your help. Come. Adam."

Colette asked one of the men, "This is very succinct. Could you please enlighten me as to what is going on? I have not heard from my family in months, and I do not know what is happening."

Colonel Scott, the highest ranking of the two men, replied, "Sure. Your brother has been involved in the Resistance for the last two years. He has become indispensable and has played a pivotal role in developing plans to liberate France. He has been going back and forth between Paris and London, carrying important information between the two cities. Last night, however, he was caught. Pierre has been trained to endure pain during interrogation. But he is only human and will not last forever. The Germans will keep him alive until they can verify that the information he gives them is correct. We have your family in hiding so they cannot be used as leverage to make him talk, and we have a plan to get him out. But it involves you. He needs you, Mrs. Walker, and so do we. If we don't get him back, many will die, and the liberation of France may have to be postponed."

The colonel took her hand in his. Colette could not believe it. She returned the secret signal and took off the apron she always wore when she worked. She thought for a moment. She could not leave George here alone. But if she did not go, her brother would die. She asked the two men to wait for a few minutes; she then found Rosie and told her the whole story.

Her friend did not hesitate. "You have to go," she said. "George will be just fine with me until you come back."

So Colette went to find her son, who was already asleep. She gently woke him up, and in a daze explained that she needed to leave for a few weeks to go help his Uncle Pierre and that she would be back in no time. He, on the other hand, needed to stay so he could help his aunt Rosie with the store and the garden until she came back. She held him tightly in his arms, kissed both his cheeks, packed a few things, and left with the two men.

"Since time is of the essence, we are going to fly you to London in a military plane. Where there is a risk of attack, you will have escorts to ensure your safety. From England, you will take a boat to Calais where you will meet with your Uncle Jules, who is also in the Resistance. He will have travel papers for you and will take you to Paris. There you will meet with his contact, who will explain to you what you need to do. Lieutenant Jones here will be with you all the way to London. Good luck. The fate of millions of people depends on you. And by the way, please know that your brothers and sisters will be watching and protecting you every step of the way. We are all proud of you."

Colette had ignored the last few sentences of his speech and thought, "No pressure...no pressure at all."

***

They flew continuously, stopping only to refuel. Occasionally she would see Allied fighter planes flying around. She had expected to see skirmishes here and there, but they arrived in London without a scratch. They had made the last part of the journey at night, so detection was even more difficult. And when she landed, Adam was waiting for her.

He kissed her on the cheek and said, "I knew you would come." He walked her to a bedroom that was located in an underground shelter. "I apologize for the accommodations. Since the Germans have been relentlessly blitzing us, we have chosen to have bedrooms underground where it is safe. By the way, you leave tomorrow night. In the meantime you can get some rest. You will find everything you need here to wash up and get comfortable. I will be back in a few minutes."

Colette ran a bath and sank into the warm water, taking her time and enjoying feeling the liquid cover her skin inch by inch. She was exhausted, and her nerves were frayed. And as promised, Adam came back within minutes. Without a word he started washing her. He rinsed her hair and body carefully and helped her out of the tub. He dried her and took her to the bed. He had intended on letting her sleep, but he had not seen her in a very long time, and she was so lovely. So he made love to her until they both fell asleep exhausted.

Colette slept most of the day. Adam woke her up around two o'clock that afternoon and helped her get ready for the trip. She was going to be taken by car to Dover where she would take a small boat to Calais. They said good-bye as she got in the car, and she never looked back. She had enough on her mind to keep her busy without thinking of her husband or the marriage she had with him.

As planned, she got on a small boat that left at sundown. And after an uneventful trip, she landed on a beach near Calais where her uncle was waiting. He kissed her soundly on both cheeks and held her in his arms for a minute before pointing toward some cabanas that lay at the edge of the beach.

"We are going to wait here for morning. A car will come and get us then, and we will travel to Paris. I have all your papers here. You know, things have changed since you left. The war has been very difficult on everyone…and your brother has been an inspiration. I thought you should know that. We are so proud of him," her uncle explained.

A few hours later, a car did arrive. Anne was at the wheel. The two women ran into each other's arms and hugged for a few seconds. They had so much to talk about, but first they had to be on their way to Paris. They would have plenty of time to catch up in the car.

The checkpoints the Germans had set up everywhere were very disturbing. When Colette had left France, her country had been free. But what was more troubling to her was that she had noticed Frenchmen working alongside the Germans. She could not understand how they could betray their country like that when others were fighting to regain France's independence.

But her uncle commented, "Don't be so harsh, Colette. Some of those men actually work for us. They help us get through the checkpoints, and they provide valuable information when they can. They are not all scum. Some actually have my respect because if they get caught, they will surely die. And some already have. That being said, since you do not know who works for us, you should never trust any of them."

He stopped for a minute and said, "Unless they give you the sign." Colette looked at her uncle a little bewildered. He continued, "Don't worry. Anne and I are Masons too. We can speak freely." Colette, who had been taught by the best, replied, "Then give me the sign, both of you."

Her uncle laughed, gave her the sign, and said, "My dear, you have been taught well. You have the right reflexes. You will do just fine. By the way, your father is running the show from his hiding place. This is why you will be dealing with people you know until we can no longer avoid bringing in strangers."

Their conversation ended when they arrived at her parents' place. She had not seen her house or her family in almost six years. She had already been told that her family had been moved to a safe house, so she was not expecting anyone. But to her surprise, her cousin Richard answered the door.

"Hello, Colette. It's so good to see you. I am your contact in Paris," said the young man.

Colette asked, "Is everyone in the family in the Resistance?"

Her cousin laughed and replied, "Well…almost…in some way or another. Thank you for bringing her here, Uncle Jules."

"You're welcome, Richard. I have to get back to Calais soon. So I wish you both the best of luck. And Colette, I will see you on your way back," said the uncle before he kissed the young people's cheeks.

Colette looked at her cousin and said, "Now what?"

Richard returned her stare and replied, "Now you put on the performance of your life. Tomorrow morning, you are going to go to the Gestapo headquarters. There you will ask to speak to Herr Schmidt. He is one of the big boss's underlings, but he can get your brother released if you play your cards right. Now, I feel very awkward asking you to do this because you are my cousin, but it is the only way. Over the next few days, and after Pierre's release, you will have to seduce Schmidt, drug him, go through his files, and steal the one on your brother. You will then kill him, come back, and take Pierre to Calais with you."

Colette was stunned. She said, "So if I understand correctly, you want me to lie, prostitute myself, steal, and kill. I have to say I was not quite expecting that. Does Adam know what you are asking of me?"

Richard waited for a moment and finally said, "Yes. He does not like it, but he knows it is the only way. And other operatives have had to do it before."

Colette replied, "The only difference is that I am not an operative. I am a healer. I save lives for a living."

Richard did not know what to say.

He looked at her for some time and finally responded, "You know, Colette, you do not have to do it. No one will hold it against you if you choose to back off."

The young woman looked at him, a little angry, and said, "But if I don't, Pierre dies. That's not much of a choice. Get me to the headquarters tomorrow, and I will get my brother out. As for the rest of your plan, we will see what I can do, but I really do not wish to kill anyone."

Her cousin became a little angry and responded, "It is so good, Colette, that you have that option. Many of us were not born killers. Yet we had to do what needed to be done for our country. I guess you do not feel the same attachment to France as we do anymore. Otherwise, we would not be having this conversation."

In a way Richard was right. She did not have the same attachment to France as he did. After all, her home was in the United States, and she had sacrificed plenty for the war there. But the living conditions were different, and she did not have to deal with combat and killings on a daily basis. She helped the injured and supported the wives and children. She organized vegetable gardens for the families in her neighborhood and healing circles for the women and children who needed help coping with the situation, but she was no killer, and she did not need to defend her home on a day-to-day basis. There was no Resistance on her turf, and she was definitely not used to having people suggest she kill anyone. She turned to her cousin and saw Anne holding him.

"There are more than war issues I am obviously not aware of," she said with a big smile. "Fill me in, you too. I have a feeling I am going to like this part of the conversation much, much more."

Anne proceeded to explain that Richard had been in her life since Colette had moved to the United States with Adam. They had gotten married two years ago in spite of the war and were both involved in the Resistance.

"Having one's neck on the line day in, day out makes for a passionate relationship," the young woman said, "when you are not out of your mind in fear that you will never see your husband again."

Colette understood these feelings all too well. But it was not of Adam that she was thinking. It was of John. Of course she would never admit this to her family. The only one who had an inkling of her deep, dark secret was Rosie.

Colette yawned. She had been up a long time. Her cousins showed her to her old room, where she would be getting her beauty sleep. She had to look her best tomorrow.

CHAPTER 9

Colette had always been exquisite. But as she strolled into the Gestapo's headquarters, she looked absolutely stunning. She walked up to the guard and said, using the softest and sexiest voice she could muster under the circumstances, "I would like to speak to Herr Schmidt as soon as possible." Still staring at her, the young man she had just spoken to placed a call and told her to go up to the second floor. The office would be the third door to her right. Had she been wearing boots, she would have been shaking in them. She was inside the building, but her heart was pounding, and a thin layer of sweat was now covering her whole body. She slowly walked up the stairs, making sure that every man in the building was aware of her presence. And everyone was.

Colette knocked at the door and walked in without even waiting for an answer. A tall blond man in his midforties who was wearing spectacles that made his Betty Blue eyes look cruel and a uniform that was so tight one might think he would pop out of it any second was standing behind the desk. He had obviously been expecting her.

But before he could utter a single word, the young woman spoke. "You must be Herr Schmidt. I have come for my brother."

"And who is your brother?" replied the German with a fake smile.

Colette looked at him and said, "I am disappointed. I thought you would know by now. My brother is Pierre Lafont."

The blond giant replied with a small laugh, "You are either crazy or stupid to come in here like this and request to have your brother back."

Colette looked at him and said, "And you, sir, must be a fool if you are thinking of turning me away without hearing me out. I have something to offer you for my brother's release. Not only can I work for you, but you can also have…me, my body, for as long as you want, for my brother's life. I really think it is a fair bargain."

The German was looking at her with interest.

She continued, "As you probably know, I have been living in the United States for the last six years. I am fluent in English, and I understand the culture that goes along with the language. But I am also French, and men trust me inherently. I can get anything out of them. You can use me to translate and even to spy. I can get information out of my brother that you will never be able to."

The German looked puzzled. "And why should I trust you?" he said.

"Because I hate Americans. My husband abused me and kidnapped my son when he left me three years ago. The American authorities have done nothing. The way I see it, if the Germans win the war, they might be able to help me, especially if I have someone of power by my side. I will not pretend to love you, because I do not know you. But I do love what you can bring me."

She paused for a few seconds and looked at him directly in the eyes. Standing tall and exposing as much cleavage as she could without popping out of her dress, she went on. "I am talking to the right man, am I not?"

The SS standing in front of her observed her for a while and said, "Take your clothes off."

Colette obliged and ever so slowly removed every piece of garment that was covering her. The German approached and raised his hand to touch her.

Colette took a step back and said, "Not so fast. First my brother, then me."

Once again the man in front of her smiled and replied, "I could take you right now, and you could not stop me."

Colette was hoping she could pull it off, and with a voice that she was barely preventing from shaking, she replied, "True. However, if you do that you will have my body once but never again. And you will never have my mind."

She approached him this time and barely touched her lips to his.

She said, "I can do things to you that you can only dream of. And I will let you do things to me that you have not yet imagined."

The soldier was under her spell. He could hardly breathe. He had to have this woman. All of her. Not just her body. He wanted to mold her into his own personal slave.

And so he said, "I will have your brother released. He will be taken to your parents'. You will stay with me so we can discuss our arrangement further."

She agreed but requested to see her brother before he left the building.

After she got dressed, she was escorted down the stairs. And when she saw her brother, her heart broke. His face was just a big red ball with slits for the eyes and lips shredded from all the beating they had sustained. There was blood trickling down his nose, which had obviously been broken. His hair was also matted with the sticky red substance. One of his arms had been broken as well, as could be seen from the unnatural angle made by the first and second half of his right forearm. And the bones in his right hand had been crushed. What she could see of his body was black and blue.

Pierre took one look at his sister and whispered, "You have to get out of here. You have no idea what they will do to you."

Colette replied with tears in her eyes, "Don't worry, little brother, I can take care of myself. I love you, and I will see you soon."

Now she understood how it was possible to kill. She truly knew hate, and she would make whomever was responsible for this horrendous treatment of Pierre pay for what they had done to him and all the other people who had suffered the same fate.

She walked back up to Herr Schmidt's office and asked, "I'm curious; whose handiwork was that?"

The German, quite satisfied with himself, replied, "If you are referring to your brother, that was my very own doing. And I will give you a taste of what came his way so you never get the idea of crossing me."

As he spoke he grabbed her, turned her around, lifted her skirt, and pulled down her panties. He bent her over on the desk, opened his own fly, spread her bottom wide, and forced himself into her rectum time and time again. Colette felt as if she was being split open. The pain was intense, and she wanted to get away. But she could not. He was holding her down and making sure she knew who the master was. Finally, he spilled his semen inside her and stopped moving. She had not made a sound. She had instinctively known that she should stay quiet if she wanted to survive this whole ordeal.

He let her go and said, "Now imagine getting that every two hours like clockwork. Go home, wash up, and come back here for dinner. If you decide not to show, I will find your brother and the rest of your family and kill them all. You have a good afternoon, my dear."

And with that he exited the room.

Colette knew what had happened was not about the sex. It was about the dominance. It was about showing who the boss was, and it was about humiliation. That German was not a man. He was a monster. She would kill him. And she would kill him soon.

She walked back home as best she could. The pain was still there, and she knew that the attack she had suffered would make it difficult for her to sit for a while. Maybe a bath would make her feel better. But first she needed to tend to her brother.

She took out the small travel kit she always had with her when she went out. She took out some herbs she had brought for bleeding and bone injuries and covered her brother's body with them. She also had him take some of the herbs in a special tea she made, as he might be bleeding internally as well. The brew relieved Pierre's pain in a matter of minutes, and he fell asleep. She took advantage of his slumber to realign his arm and brace it so the bones would not move. She would never forget his face when she had walked in the door. He had not been able to speak. He had just cried when he had seen his sister walk in. He knew what she had just been through for him. He knew the pain and the humiliation firsthand, and he wished there was something he could do to protect her. Instead she had given him the respite he needed to get his strength back and go on.

He woke up a few hours later, as Colette was getting ready. Richard was giving her instructions, but she was barely listening. She was planning her revenge. He could tell. And he would not blame her. The young men had known Colette their whole lives. They both knew that there was no point in telling her what to do. They knew she would bring the file back and that she would kill Herr Schmidt. How she did it was really up to her. She had the sleeping potion that she could put in his drink if she felt she needed to use it. But from the looks of things, she already had a plan—and a mean one at that. Richard just hoped she did not lose her soul in the process.

***

Colette took her travel kit with her when she returned to Herr Schmidt, and over dinner she had broached the subject of how to increase sexual pleasure with acupuncture needles. She told him that she had trained with a shaolin master in the United States and that part of the training had been on harnessing sexual energy. She went on to explain that the needles made the experience even more powerful. The legend that accompanied the practice mentioned that the recipient of such a treatment was given magical powers that would allow him to control his own destiny. The SS officer grew excited just thinking about the possibilities. Colette then suggested they go back to his office since it was the closest place where they could try this ancient, and oh-so-secret, technique.

Since the German officer was a little anxious about being needled, Colette showed him on her own arm what it entailed. Relieved that the process was so simple, he agreed to take his clothes off and lie down on the sofa facedown. Colette inserted a couple of needles in his back, and once her prey was completely reassured that all was well, she introduced a needle at the base of his skull. But instead of pointing the needle up toward the nose, she angled it down toward the medulla oblongata, the small part of the brain responsible for breathing, heart rate, and muscle movement, among other things. She had used the biggest and longest needle she had and inserted it very gently. She then pretended to be stimulating the point, moving the needle to and fro. She felt the strong German go limp, and soon he started gasping for air. She went in front of him so he could see her face. He looked like a goldfish that had just jumped out of his bowl. He tried to no avail to move his arms to remove the needle.

Colette smiled and said, "And now, I am going to watch you die. I want you to remember the pain you have inflicted on so many. I want you to remember my brother and me. Should I sodomize you the way you did us just before you die? I think not. I will just leave you like that so your underlings have the pleasure of finding out that you have been murdered by the woman you wanted to enslave. But I will wait here with you until you take your last breath. I want to be sure the job is done right. And while you take your sweet time dying, I will look in your desk for the file on my brother. And here it is! You are so organized. Thank you. It really made my job much easier."

She really did not want to hang around. Now that she had the file, she wanted it over with. She had seen the fear in his eyes, but she had not seen remorse, and she knew she never would. So she took the letter opener that was on the man's desk and plunged it in alongside the needle. The German jerked once and finally closed his eyes. She checked his vitals. He was dead. She was free to go.

She made her exit from the Gestapo headquarters and walked back to her parents' place. There she took her belongings, her brother, and the car her cousin had left for her escape. She put her brother in the trunk after having prepared a big batch of herbs for the trip. She would not see her family, but she had to get her brother out of there fast. She needed to be on the boat back to England before eight o'clock the next morning. They had to be gone before the corpse was discovered.

She drove all night, went through a few checkpoints, and explained each time that she was a doctor and that she was meeting her aunt who was gravely ill. They let her go every time. But when she was almost home free, the guard on duty asked her if she could open the trunk for him. She slowly came out of the car, taking time to assess the situation, when one of the French patrols came to suggest that his colleague go in for a well-deserved drink. The German soldier gladly went in, and the French one opened the trunk. He looked at Colette, closed it right back, and said, "You are free to go. Have a safe trip."

Colette was on the boat with her brother ten minutes later. She had had just enough time to kiss her uncle good-bye. A storm was rolling in, and it would be a rough ride, but they could not wait until the weather cleared. So they left the safety of the beach and braved the roaring sea. Pierre was sick within the first fifteen minutes of leaving the shore, so Colette once again took her needles out to take care of the motion sickness. She inserted a needle in each of her brother's wrists, and soon the nausea disappeared.

But the waves were getting bigger and bigger by the minute. They would not make it to England if the storm kept on badgering the poor boat. Fear gripped at her throat. So instinctively she went to what she knew. If she could control energy to treat her patients and affect their surroundings, she might be able to do the same to hers on a much larger scale. So Colette concentrated on surrounding the boat with her own energy, molding it into white light, and thus establishing a safe passage for them all. She also visualized them in London. To her great surprise, the boat settled down a little. For sure she must be imagining things. But every time she stopped her visualization, the boat would start its mad dance again. So she continued. She thought that if it was not helping, it certainly would not hurt.

Finally, as the sun was rising, they landed in Dover. She had made it. Her brother was safe. His file was in good hands, and soon she could go home. A car was waiting for them to take them back to London. To her surprise, Lieutenant Jones was waiting for her. He said, "Welcome back, Mrs. Walker. And congratulations on a job well done. You will rest for a few days, and we will fly you back to the States if that is what you wish. But you know, we could use someone like you full-time."

Colette replied, "I thank you for your kind offer, Lieutenant, but I have a son waiting for me at home who needs his mother. It just would not do if I died in this war. I do intend to see him fully grown, married, and with children of his own."

The officer smiled understandingly. He wished he had that option. He would have loved to see his wife and kids. He then turned to Pierre. "And welcome to you, M. Lafont. We have been eager to get you back. Thanks to your sister, we do expect you to make a full recovery. Your hand will be the hardest for us to repair, but our best surgeons are ready to work on you."

Over the next few days, Colette took advantage of her time on base with her brother to give him all the treatments she could manage with her limited equipment. She was also asked to report on how she had gotten the information and escaped in the end. It was painful to go over those events in her mind again, but it also somehow seemed to have a therapeutic effect. She would always bear the trauma of what had happened to her and what she had done. But sharing the burden seemed to make it less heavy on her own mind. Now she was ready to go home.

She said good-bye to her brother and walked to the plane that had been assigned to take her back to the States. She had not seen Adam, and she got a strange feeling in the pit of her stomach. But she was eager to leave and set this feeling aside.

Before the plane took off, a man in a gray suit walked up to her. He shook her hand, gave her the signal, and asked to talk to her privately. "I'm Michael Bates I wanted to thank you personally for what you have done. Your bravery has saved many lives. And in spite of the fact that you are a woman, you are a true Mason. I know that you want to go home. But I want you to consider the possibility of working with us again if need be." Colette did not know if she should be flattered or offended. The British really needed to understand that women were at least as valuable as men in all aspects of life. But she said nothing. She just smiled and walked back to the plane. All she wanted to do was see her son.

As she sat down in the passenger seat, she introduced herself to the pilot. And when she shook his hand, chills traveled down her spine. She had this odd feeling that something was definitely off, as if this young man should not be flying this mission. But instead of sharing her feelings with him, she told herself that she was just nervous about flying, and that was all. Yet the uneasiness did not go away.

CHAPTER 10

They had been flying for a while, and the pilot looked worried.

He finally said, "Tonight may not be as quiet as your previous trip. The Germans are on alert. They have been flying a lot more and are looking for any reason to engage us. Let's hope we make it past Norway so we can refuel in Iceland."

Another five tense minutes went by before they saw flashes of light.

"Shit, they have found us. They are shooting at us. Those darn Germans. Never are where they should be. At home," the young man said. He continued speaking, leading the plane in a feverish waltz through the air as if it were a feather tossed around by the wind. "We are not going to get out of this one. Another two planes are joining this one. We are going to go down eventually. I will do my best to keep you safe. But in case something happens to me, here is my pistol. You arm it this way, you aim, and you shoot directly to the heart. Brace yourself for the recoil, and you will be fine."

Colette was scared out of her mind. All she could think about was George…and John. She had to make it out alive, no matter what. No matter what, she kept thinking to herself. She had already killed a man and may have to kill another, if that meant she could see her son again. Her nightmarish daydreaming was interrupted by the sudden dive of the plane. The pilot had been hit but was still able to exert some influence on the plane. The sheer terror that went through Colette in those few seconds was probably the most intense she had ever felt. She did not want to die. She could not die. The plane was getting closer to the ground. It was going to crash, and there was nothing she could do.

She woke up coughing, smelling the toxic fumes of burning paint. The pilot was lying next to her, looking like a ragged doll. His leg was visibly broken, and there was blood all over his face. His eyes were open, and he was not breathing. Realizing that he was dead and that the plane she was leisurely sitting in could blow up any second, Colette grabbed her travel kit and the gun the young man had given her and ran for cover in a nearby patch of trees.

She had been sitting with her back to a big pine tree when she heard voices. She had been blaming herself for the pilot's life. She should have told him. Maybe he would have chosen not to fly this mission. But instead she made the choice for him. She really had had no right. And then she heard them. Three German soldiers were approaching the wreckage. Colette stopped breathing. The last thing she needed was to get caught by the Germans. The news of her actions in Paris might not have made it all the way to Norway, but she was bound to appear on a list of wanted people sooner or later. In spite of the cold, she was sweating. Her hair was matted to her head. Not once did she consider that she had bumped her head during the crash and that the matting was due to the caked blood and not the sweat. She was holding the gun, ready to shoot, if any of the men got closer.

And after a thorough investigation, the soldiers, satisfied that the dead pilot was the only one present in the cockpit at the time of the crash, finally left the scene. Colette breathed a sigh of relief. She had escaped unseen. She was cold, however, and needed some shelter. She had no idea where she was and needed to make a decision soon as to what she was going to do, as forest survival was not her forte. Besides she had people to see and places to go.

She very carefully went back to the plane to see if there was anything she could salvage. Unfortunately, everything of value had been removed by the three visitors. So she opted to go south. After all, it was as good a direction as any. She was cold, and in her mind the south had always been associated with warmth. She knew that finding any type of non-German civilization was a long shot, but she had to try. She found the North Star in the sky and went in the opposite direction. She hoped it would be light soon. She knew she was close to the coast. If she was indeed going in the right direction, she would see the sun rise to her left.

After hours of uninterrupted walking, she saw some smoke rising from the chimney of an old wooden farmhouse. In spite of the late morning hour, the light was still scarce. Dark, gray clouds obstructed the sun. She decided to get closer to see who lived there. But when she got to the window, she felt an object push on her back. A man spoke to her in Norwegian. She did not understand a thing and told him just so. She suggested French or English.

In a most pleasing English, the Norwegian replied, "Where do you come from, and how did you get to my house?"

Colette explained her situation and begged him not to turn her in.

"I have no intention of turning you in. I will figure out what to do with you later. But first you will have to lie low for a while. The Germans are bound to be looking for you," replied the stranger.

"As a matter of fact, they will not. I saw them search the plane. They did not find any indication that I was ever in there. Otherwise they would have done a thorough search of the area right on the spot," answered Colette.

They walked into the house, where the warmth instantly enveloped the young woman. She felt as if a nice heavy wool blanket had been deposited on her shoulders on a snowy winter night. Now that the lights were on, she could study her rescuer a little closer. He was a tall, blond man with blue eyes, and he was in his early forties, it seemed.

Noticing the scrutinizing look Colette was sending his way, he said, "My name is Agnar. What's yours?"

The young woman answered his question while he prepared what appeared to be a hot drink.

He continued, "Here, have some glogg. It's mulled wine, and it will warm you up. Now let me wash your face and take a look at the gash on your head. It's probably not too bad, but it will need cleaning."

Only then did Colette remember the matted hair on her head. She had had no time to pay attention to a little detail like that, but now she was a bit concerned. She asked for a mirror and some water. She also explained that she practiced Oriental medicine in the United States and that she had some herbs with her that might take care of the problem.

Once she had cleaned her face and head, the bleeding started again. This type of injury would have required stitches, but she could not afford to be seen. So once again, the herbs would have to do. She had a little bit of Yunnan Baiyao powder left. She instructed Agnar to sprinkle some on the wound. Within a few minutes, the bleeding had stopped and a crusty scab appeared in place of the gash. The Norwegian was quite impressed. He then showed her to a room where she could rest peacefully.

She still looked worried, so he said, "Don't fret. I will not let anything happen to you. We will figure out how to get you home."

Agnar walked back downstairs and waited to listen to the daily news on the radio. At the same time every evening, the Norwegian Resistance would give out messages to its members over the air. And tonight would be no different. Except for one thing. This time the message was for him. It was coded so any interception by the Germans would be useless. And upon translation it said, "A plane crashed in your area. Intelligence reports said that the pilot died. However, there is no mention of the woman that was accompanying him. Find her and take her to Baldur for extraction."

This woman must be connected, he thought, in order to have an extraction team ready to get her out even before the day was over. He woke her up with the news and told her to get ready to meet with the man mentioned in the message. Agnar had heard of him but had never met him. He would have to be very careful to leave her in the right hands. And when Colette had gathered her meager belongings, they left.

Agnar drove for about thirty minutes with Colette on the floor in the back of the truck. He had covered her with blankets and hay so she looked like a big lump of animal feed.

Once they reached Baldur's farm, he knocked at the door and said, "I brought some hay for your animal. Where would you like me to put it?"

The other man replied, "Go to the back of the house. There is a shed. You can store it there."

Once again Agnar followed instructions.

But once he was out back, he said, "You are not going to leave the girl here all night, are you?"

The other man snickered and replied, "Of course not. You do not do this very often, do you. Go home now."

Agnar would not leave until he knew Colette was safe. So Baldur grabbed Colette's hand and gave a sign. Colette smiled and looked at Agnar.

"Thank you so much for saving my life. I will never forget it. And hopefully we will meet again someday…under better circumstances," she said as she kissed his cheek.

Agnar left, and Colette turned to Baldur. "Wow, we really are everywhere. When I was told there would always be a Freemason close by to lend a hand if I needed it, I had no idea that extended to the middle of Norway in wartime."

"Even more so in wartime than at any other time, my dear sister, as most of us are engaged in the Resistance or the war effort in some way," he replied.

Baldur was an older man with a kind face. He was wearing spectacles and looked more like a university professor than a Resistance fighter. And that was exactly what made him the perfect choice for this mission. He was to take Colette by boat to a rendezvous point on the North Sea. There she would meet with a British war vessel that would take her to Iceland. From there she would fly back to New York, where she would meet her mother-in-law and eventually take the train back to the West Coast. It was a failsafe plan, except for the meeting in waters under German surveillance.

But Baldur would pull it off. With the help of his nephew, who owned a fishing boat, he put Colette in the fish storage container until it was time to go the next morning. Once on the way, his nephew started fishing so they could throw a blanket of fresh fish over the young woman. Colette was not very happy with the plan, until the small boat was stopped by a German patrol vessel that was protecting the coast of Norway. One of the officers asked to check the fishing boat for contraband. He looked into the compartment Colette was hiding in. And since he only saw fish, he was satisfied that the craft could complete its fishing trip.

They eventually reached the British ship—a few minutes late but unharmed. Colette was transferred and thanked her brother for all his help. Once more she hoped she would meet him again under better circumstances. She watched the fishing boat sail away, and then she walked back to a young man who appeared to be waiting for her.

"I would appreciate any type of clothing that would allow me to change into something that does not smell like sardines. And if you had a freshwater basin I could wash up with, I would be eternally grateful," she commented.

The man smiled and replied, "Sure thing, Mrs. Walker. But so you know, you really do not smell that bad."

"Thank you, young man," she returned with a smile. She continued, "Nonetheless, I would rather not wear a perfume that would make all the cats in New York follow my every move"

***

Colette arrived in New York as she had done once before with Adam. She was now a US citizen, so the entry into the country was a lot easier, particularly since she entered by plane. She was indeed escorted by the air force pilot who had flown her back in. Within minutes she was outside hugging her mother-in-law and the rest of the family. She wanted to rest, but she also wanted to hear all that they had to tell her about their life in New York. Things had changed with the war, but New York was New York.

And for the next few days, she almost forgot there was a war. She ate decent food and enjoyed the long walks and talks she had with her in-laws. She even took the time to soak in a nice warm bath for an hour. She felt pampered and loved. She was wanted— so much so, that when she talked about going home to her son, her in-laws suggested she send for him so they could live in New York with them. As tempting as it sounded, Colette knew she had to go back. Rosie needed her, and so did her patients. She had to go back.

***

Colette got out of the car just in front of Rosie's store. She could not wait to see her son again.

"Hi, Rosie," she said as she hugged her friend. "Where is George?" she asked.

Her friend replied, "He is in bed. He started running a fever last night. I'm so happy you're back. Go take a look at him. And by the way, he is not the only one. A lot of kids are coughing and running fevers, and the parents are asking about you."

Colette ran to her son and listened to his lungs. She took his temperature, palpated the neck area, looked in his ears and nose, and said, "I think it's pneumonia. I will go prepare some herbs so he can start taking them right away. Then I will go check on the others. Do you have a list of the sick kids?"

Rosie provided the names of the families who had asked for her help, and Colette started her rounds. She would have loved to bathe and take a nap, but the situation required immediate attention. The longer her patients remained without treatment, the more difficult the illness would be to eradicate, and the more complications might arise. So she saw one patient after the next. And when she finally got home, it was way past midnight.

She had not slept in what seemed like days, but she checked on George before she went to bed. Thankfully, the fever had abated. George would be fine, and so would her other little patients. For some reason, only the children seemed to have been affected by this disease. She had recommended that everyone wash their hands thoroughly a few times a day, to use a scarf to cover their mouths when they were around sick children, and to stay away from coughing people as much as possible. That might help with curbing the epidemic.

CHAPTER 11

On August 15, 1945, the war finally ended. Europe had been liberated, and Japan had just surrendered. Colette decided right then and there that she was moving back to her own home. Her friend Rosie was becoming more and more involved with Harold, and it was time to give her some space. Besides, the restrictions would probably end soon.

Colette had not heard from Adam in spite of easier communication between the two continents. But she had received a letter from her family. They missed her terribly, but everyone was fine. They had all survived. Even Pierre. His hands had healed, and so had the rest of his body. Colette wondered about his soul. What he had gone through was bound to have left some deep-seated marks. She wished she could see him again.

On the other hand, John had stopped writing entirely, and Colette was extremely worried. She knew that only his parents would be advised should anything happen to him. After all the tenants who had lived next door to her had been drafted, no one had moved in. The house had remained vacant for four years. She was not sure whether John's belongings had been removed. She had never seen anyone come by. So she wondered every day if he was still alive.

Some of the less injured men were starting to come back. The women and children were smiling again, and Colette was busy tending to the ones needing medical attention. One day, when she had just finished dressing a minor wound that had had a difficult time healing, she felt a presence staring at her. She raised her head to see who was there and stopped in her tracks. She was paralyzed. In front of her, John stood with his hand holding a cane.

He was intently looking at her and said, "I'm going to need your expertise to get back on my feet, Doctor."

She ran to him, tears of joy in her eyes, and almost knocked him over.

"You came back," she said in a barely audible voice.

"Told you I would. I always keep my promises," he replied, and he gave her the biggest smile he could muster.

Colette was hugging him so hard he could scarcely breathe. And then she started sobbing. She did not care who saw her. She only cared that he was alive, that he had come back to her. The relief she felt was so intense that she almost collapsed. But, thankfully, with his one free arm John was holding her as tightly as she was holding on to him.

Once she recovered a little, Colette had him sit down in a private area and looked at his leg. The wound was not so bad and was actually healing nicely. All he would need was a little acupuncture to loosen the tissue around the scar and alleviate the pain until he was completely recuperated.

As she was working on him, he asked, "How is Adam?"

Colette told him that she had no idea where he was or whether he was still alive. She then asked John what his plans were and was informed that he was going back to school to complete his engineering degree. He only had one year left, and his parents insisted he do it, in spite of the fact that he could have gone to work in one of their stores.

While Colette was working on him, John wanted to touch her, to take her in his arms, to tell her how much he loved her and how much her letters had helped to keep him alive. She had given him hope. She had given him the will to come back. But he had other news for her as well. When he had returned to his parents, he found out that they had arranged for him to marry a Chinese girl from San José. His fiancée's parents and his own had been business associates for a long time, and the union would be profitable to both families. But how could he marry someone he did not love, especially when he loved another? How could he find the courage to tell Colette that he would marry someone else? The wedding was set for July 1946, one month after his graduation. But since he was a man of honor, he told Colette.

Her worst fear had materialized. He had come back to her, but she would lose him to another. She thought that she had no right to expect anything else from him and told him so. She wanted him to be happy, and she knew from watching him with George that he would be a great father.

She smiled and said, "I do hope your wife and I will be friends. I never want you out of my life again. You are my best friend."

***

John was waiting for Colette and her son just outside of the house. It had been a few days since he had last seen her, and they had agreed to go on a picnic. The weather was still nice, and they had wanted to take advantage of the last few days of the Indian summer.

George was the first to come out, and he ran to John to take his hand. Colette followed, wearing one of her old floral dresses. Even in this old thing, she looked amazing. She had not changed one bit. She was still as desirable as the day he had left. There was, however, a little something in her eyes that he could not quite put his finger on. He had found out from Rosie that she had cared for the community for months on her own. The old doctor had passed away, and the young ones were all fighting this nasty war.

But it was more than that. There was a new seriousness to her, even a sadness that lingered that was not there before. He would have to find out what it was. As this last thought entered his mind, he noticed the perfect tree for their outing. It was tall and leafy, just the appropriate size to protect them from the sun. And it was surrounded by a nice lawn where George could play and run to his heart's content.

The food Colette had prepared was delicious as usual. She had made a rice salad with tomatoes, olives, eggs, and vinaigrette. She had also baked a cake for dessert and brought some apples for them to snack on in the afternoon. As she bent over to cut the cake, a welcome gust of wind placed a lock of her hair on her mouth. Wanting to be helpful, John attempted to remove the offending lock. He succeeded in his mission, but also triggered a chain reaction that stopped them in their tracks. The electricity that passed between them was palpable. They exchanged a look that told them of the coming torture. Their casual touching would forever generate a need that could never be quenched.

For John, the need to be near her was so great that when he touched her hand, his felt as if it had been set on fire. For Colette, the skin John had barely touched tingled and burned for hours after contact. Yet they could not stay away from each other. It was always the most innocent of touches on the outside, but the fantasies it elicited in them were far from that.

In his head their lovemaking was always so very tender...He wanted to make her happy. He imagined himself touching the white skin of her neck and caressing every inch of her body. He wanted to kiss the hollow of her back and lift her long hair to have access to the delicate skin at the nape of her neck. He wanted to feel her breasts in his hands and take them in his mouth until she couldn't stand it anymore. He wanted to put his head between her legs and give her the pleasure she deserved. He wanted to have her beg for him to take her. And finally he wanted to have her body and soul.

John had to snap out of it, and fast. Otherwise Colette would quickly notice where his mind had been for the last few seconds. But it was always the same, except for the need that was growing stronger. They really should have asked Rosie and her friend to join them. At least the intimacy would have been reduced and the day would have been a little less threatening for his sanity, as well as his pants.

***

John had always been mature for his age, but the war had changed him. He had always been a man in Colette's eyes, but there was an added wisdom to him since he had come back that made him even more attractive. He was even kinder and gentler with her, but he also seemed to know what he wanted a lot more. And Colette could feel that he wanted her. She could see it in his eyes sometimes. And when he touched her, sparks flew. She had to constantly apply herself not to let her mind wander into unauthorized territories. She had to remind herself every minute that she was a married woman, even if she was married to the wrong man. The agony she was feeling as she denied herself the pleasures she was sure to experience with John was becoming more and more physical. She had had a taste of it once before the war. It had only been a kiss, but it was the kiss of a lifetime. They had poured all their emotions, their love for each other, and their sorrow for what was to come into that one perfect kiss. She had no regrets, but she knew it could never happen again.

Colette had confided in Rosie to get her friend's opinion on the situation, and the answer she obtained was a very simple one. "Get a divorce from Adam, and marry John," Rosie had said. It was really that simple. Except it really was not. Only the less honorable members of society divorced. And they were really frowned upon. Besides, she had a child, and she had been raped, not to mention the fact that she had killed a man. And Asian families wanted their males to marry virgins with no life experience; a young wife would be expected to do her husband's and mother-in-law's bidding without question. And that she was not. So marrying John would never be an option even if she chose to divorce eventually. And there was another little problem. As of today, she had no idea where her husband was. She had not received any notice from the army, so she assumed he was still alive. But that was not much to go on to start any legal proceedings—if that was indeed what she was going to do. Regardless, she would always be John's friend and nothing more. But the following morning, she would write her mother-in-law to find out if she had heard from Adam.

***

Colette had invited her friends over for dinner. Rosie and Harold, who had just gotten engaged, arrived first. They had brought a bottle of wine from the nearby Napa Valley. The groom-to-be was struggling to open it when John finally joined them. They all toasted the newly betrothed couple and continued their celebration over the wonderful meal Colette had prepared yet again.

From the asparagus mousse to the apple pie, which Colette made French style without cinnamon, the meal was a success. And in spite of Colette's refusal, everyone cleared the table and helped wash the dishes. Then they all landed on the sofa to enjoy a nice glass of brandy. There were laughs and fun conversation. It had been, for all intents and purposes, a real celebration. And after the austerity of the war, it felt really good to be able to laugh again.

But as all good things come to an end, the bride- and groom-to-be bade their hostess good-bye and left hand in hand. And John followed suit. Colette was a little disappointed as she had hoped they would have a little time alone, but she knew it was for the best. So she went back to the kitchen and decided to take the garbage out. The back alley, as usual, was enveloped in darkness at that late hour, so Colette did not notice that a man was standing in the bushes. As she was about to dump her trash in the appropriate container, he grabbed her and forced her into his hiding place. Colette screamed as loudly as she could. She kicked him and threw the full bucket of trash onto the man's head. He lost his footing long enough for the young woman to escape and run back toward her house. Halfway there, she collided with John, who had heard her scream and was coming to rescue her. She briefly explained where her assailant was, but by the time the young man got there, the perpetrator had vanished.

Colette had gone inside the house as instructed and was waiting for John. It seemed as if an eternity had gone by before he came back. But when he finally arrived, Colette started sobbing. She had been so afraid. She had done what she needed to do to survive, thinking only of George. She had fought with all her strength to make sure her little boy would still have a mother when he woke up.

John could not stand the sight of her crying. Her dress was torn at the shoulder, and he knew that Colette had escaped in the nick of time. He was so proud of her for keeping her cool and getting out unharmed. He would not have forgiven himself had anything happened to her. As he shuddered at the thought, he reached for her and pulled him into his arms. He would teach George and her the martial arts his father had taught him so they could defend themselves from other assailants.

He held her until their bodies felt as if they had melted together. And ever so gently, he raised her chin with his free hand so she would look at him. And then he was lost. His mouth covered hers with such passion that Colette lost her balance. John's strong arms prevented her from falling, and he deposited her on the sofa where they had enjoyed their brandy earlier that night. Without even stopping his kiss, he did what he had dreamed of doing for years. Ever so slowly, as if not to scare her away, he let one of his hands trace a line from her jaw to her breasts. And when he finally touched her budding nipple, he felt her drain all the air around them as she gasped. He touched all the parts of her body he could reach easily as their kiss deepened. The world around them did not exist anymore. Their obligations were no longer at the forefront of their mind. She was touching him too and setting him on fire. If they did not stop soon, there would be no turning back. The fog that had descended on their minds made it impossible to think, and the alcohol they had consumed removed the last bits of inhibition they might have had.

But as suddenly as the kiss had started, Colette stopped and looked at him with tears in her eyes and said, "As much as I love you, John, I am still married to another man, and until that changes, if it ever does, I cannot give myself to you."

With a sad little smile, John got up and left.

The next morning, the young man started their martial arts training. They agreed to meet twice a week for lessons. George and Colette would practice together every day after work. And John knew that in no time they would master the basics. They seemed to be naturals at it, and it made him feel better. He knew that they would not be able to fight effectively for some time, but they would know enough to be able to escape from any situation. And for now, that was enough.

CHAPTER 12

Colette had not seen John in a few days, but she had had the feeling recently that something was about to happen. She had asked the United States government about her husband's whereabouts, as her mother-in-law had not heard from him either and had been told that he was still stationed in Europe. One morning, as Colette picked up her mail, she immediately saw an envelope with her husband's handwriting. Hands shaking, she opened it to find this note:

Dear Colette,

It looks like I will be in France for the next few years. I have found the love of my life there, and I have decided to marry her. I have contacted an attorney in the United States who will take care of our divorce. Please sign the enclosed papers. I leave you sole custody of George as I know I will have no time to take care of him. And since you have fended for yourself so well during the war, I know you will not need me at all to raise him. I wish you the best.

Adam

Colette started to cry. Part of her was relieved that this farce of a marriage was finally over. But part of her grieved for the little boy who would have no father, and she knew that from now on she would be both to him forever. Maybe one day, George would want to see Adam, and if that ever occurred, she would make it happen. After all, Colette had survived so much already, she could keep going alone.

With that in mind, she ran to Rosie's and told her the bittersweet news. She was now free, but she was also a divorcée, part of a group that was really comprised of outcasts in this society. But as her friend reminded her, she was also a white Frenchwoman practicing Chinese medicine in a country that was not her own. And that made her even more unusual.

Colette decided she would not tell John if she saw him again. Well, maybe she would, if she found the courage. She was embarrassed to have been so foolish when she had married Adam. And she was even more embarrassed to bring the stigma of the divorced parent upon her child. There were so many important things she had not told John…What was one more, after all?

George had been without a father for so long that the idea of Adam remaining in France was just fine. Besides, he liked John better. They were buddies. They played together often, and John would come to take him to the park every Wednesday after he finished school. George did not really remember much of his father, except that sometimes his mother was not happy when they lived together. Well, it was more of a feeling than really remembering, or at least that was what Colette had gathered from her son's simple words after she had told him the news. She had not told him the whole truth. She had not mentioned that his father had walked out on him, that he did not care if he ever saw him again. She had kept quiet about the fact that Adam did not even feel he was responsible for the financial well-being of his child. Instead she had told her son that his father loved him but that he had to stay in France to help with the reconstruction after the war. She had said that any time he wanted to hear from his father, he could telegram him and Adam would respond right away. She had explained that she and Adam would go their separate ways, but that they both remained his parents forever. The little boy had just acknowledged and gone back to the game he was playing, seemingly unaffected by his mother's revelations.

***

The following Wednesday, John came to pick George up to take him to the park. He chatted with Colette about little nothings and soon left with the child. But when he came back an hour later, John looked upset. As a matter of fact, Colette had never seen him this way. Her friend was fuming, angry beyond words, and so mad he was beet red. So she sent George to play in the backyard. She offered the young man a cup of coffee, as she had just made some. She served John a cup and sat at the kitchen table across from him.

He was staring at the blue-and-white squares of the tablecloth when he finally said, "Why didn't you tell me? George told me you have known for some time that Adam was not coming back."

"It has just been a few days," Colette replied, "and I really did not know how to tell you. Besides, it changes nothing. I am still a woman with a child, not a virgin, and a divorcée to boot."

John was becoming more and more agitated. "You know I don't care about all that. You are now free," he retorted.

"But you are not!" she snapped right back. "You are getting married in a few months to a woman who will make you happy," she finished.

"That could change," John retorted.

"No, it cannot," Colette said. "You do not know everything that happened during the war. I went back to France for a few weeks to help my brother, who had been taken prisoner, and in the process, I was raped, and I killed the man who did it. So you see, John, I am damaged goods. I am not the wife for you."

John was absolutely stunned. But in the fog that was now enveloping his every thought he managed to ask, "Colette, please start from the beginning and tell me everything."

The young woman obliged and shared with him the darkest moments of her life.

John could not believe that Adam had asked that of Colette. He must have known that something like that would happen. He was furious…and sad…very sad. He had not been there to protect her. And she had survived, but he knew that deep down a little part of her had died in France the day she rescued her brother. No woman should have ever had to live through this. And the fact that her own husband had thrown her into the enemy's claws without a second look was just plain sickening. And for some reason, he loved her even more. She probably was the most courageous woman he had ever met, and he wanted her, body and soul.

He knew that his fiancée would never make him happy. He had met her, courted her, and even kissed her once. And nothing happened. No sparks. No knees made of jelly. No unbearable feeling that he wanted to make love to her on the spot. It felt as if he was kissing his mother or his sister. As a matter of fact, it really was a little disgusting, and thus he had never done it again. With that in mind, he could not even come close to envisioning a lifetime of intimacy with the woman his parents had picked out for him. He knew he had no choice. His parents had chosen for him and had pledged him to his wife-to-be. And according to Chinese culture, he had to obey. But he could only think of Colette. She was free now, and he did not care about the rest. Besides, he loved George too, as if the child was his own. There had to be a way to salvage their lives and make them happy for the rest of their days. George deserved to have a father who really loved him and Colette a husband who could spoil her forever.

***

Since John and Colette had both been invited to Rosie and Harold's wedding, they had agreed to go together. Colette was the maid of honor and he the best man. So he came to pick her up a few hours before the ceremony so she could be with Rosie to help her get ready and so he could make sure that Harold did not get cold feet. And as Colette walked out the front door, she took his breath away. She looked like an angel. The pale pink of her dress brought out the soft blush on her cheeks and made her skin look like velvety cream. The empire waist showed off her generous breast, while the breeze pulled the fabric close to her body to reveal her perfect curves. Her hair was up in a bun, but some tendrils had escaped and cascaded to her shoulders like a frame around her exquisite heart-shaped face. Her eyes glowed with pride, as she knew she looked like a fairytale princess. And they were blue, so blue. It seemed that day as if the sky had matched their color. The only jewelry she wore were pearl earrings and a little silver moon pendant that her mother had sent her the previous Christmas.

George, in his Sunday best, was running along in front of them. John had offered his arm to Colette, who had taken it gracefully. They walked together, quiet, and happy just to be, for a moment. And when they reached Rosie's, they separated to tend to their duties as expected.

When the bride and groom were ready, the ceremony started. The music was playing, and John took Colette into the church. They walked side by side and waited for the bride and groom to arrive. They could not take their eyes off each other. The reverend was speaking, but it did not matter. What was important was that they were together under this holy roof. And they were both thinking that it could be them had things been different, had they met sooner, somehow.

Colette, in addition to her other duties as maid of honor, had offered to prepare the wedding dinner. The guests raved about its quality. The little puff pastries were divine, and the beef Wellington was cooked to perfection. And Colette had outdone herself with the cake too. With John's help, who had carved a bride and a groom out of wood, she had been able to make a *pièce montée* with beautiful golden cream puffs rising in a pyramid of sweetness and culminating with the wooden newlyweds. It looked professionally made, and Colette was happy with the result. She had cooked for days to prepare for the event, and her friends were ecstatic. She had wanted to give them the perfect wedding, so that was all that mattered. They were like family to her.

The first dance was announced, and Rosie and Harold obliged the crowd. Then the dance floor filled with people, and John offered Colette his hand. He took her to the center of the action, and they danced in each other's arms all night. It was magical. Once again they were transported to a world that only they inhabited. But too soon, the music stopped, and Cinderella had to go home to continue her regular daily life.

It had been a wonderful day that she would remember and cherish for the rest of her life. John walked her home. They had had a little to drink and were laughing, discussing the night's events and the merits of marriage, when Colette turned to him and said, "If I ever remarry, I will make sure that my husband is gentle and pleasures me to orgasm. Otherwise, what is the point? I have a child, and I take care of myself financially. I really don't need a man."

John smiled. He admired her forthcoming and honest way of saying what she meant. And she was right. She deserved a good man to take care of her, and he hoped she would have that someday.

John kissed her cheek to say good-bye and then slowly touched his lips to hers. He had promised himself he would not do it, but he had to taste her one more time, feel the connection they would always have. It was pure torture. It was heaven. And hell. Her lips were so soft and willing. He pulled back using all the strength he could muster and promised to stop by soon. Colette watched him leave, in a daze, wondering what had happened. She finally went inside and walked up the stairs to put George to bed. But to her surprise, the poor little guy was already asleep, fully dressed, on his bed. She took his clothes off without even waking him. He had had a very busy day and had enjoyed himself immensely. She then went to her own room, got into her favorite cotton nightgown, and brushed her hair. She had decided she would get into bed and relive the day's events. It had been such a beautiful day. But she was so exhausted by the time she actually hit the pillow that she fell into a deep sleep until well into the next morning.

CHAPTER 13

It was time for John to do some serious shopping. Tonight, he would go to his future in-laws and present his bride-to-be with her engagement ring. He would then get on one knee and officially ask her to marry him. He had no idea where to start, so he went to Colette's. She might be able to help him. He had to tell her what he was about to do. He felt she had the right to know. And that would be even more time he could spend with her.

He rang the doorbell and waited patiently for her to open the door. When she finally did, her hair was all wet. She was obviously just out of the tub.

Images he should have fought started swarming his overly creative mind.

"Get your head out of the gutter," he told himself. "Stay close to the subject at hand. Colette deserves this much."

He walked past her and stood by the stairs to the upstairs bedrooms. He looked at her and waited for her to say something. And she finally did.

"You obviously came here to tell me something of importance. I can see it on your face," she said.

However, she could not quite figure out what he needed to discuss so badly. The last time she had seen a similar expression was the day he told her he had been drafted. But the war had ended, so that was out. She wondered how long he was going to keep silent.

"I am going to make my parents proud tonight. I am officially getting engaged. As a matter of fact, I have to go get the ring right now. I have been procrastinating, but now I have to get it done. Come with me. I need your strength," John begged.

Colette could not believe what this man was asking of her. If she understood correctly, he wanted her to help him choose the ring that would tie him to another woman forever. Was he out of his mind? How did he expect her to make it through the day? But she had said she would be his friend always, and that is what friends did. They helped each other. John had always been there for her. He had saved George's life. Hell, he had even held her hand through labor. What he was asking of her was minor in comparison. So she said yes.

She grabbed her purse, dropped George off at Rosie's, and went to San Francisco with John. The first jewelry store they stopped at was not very pleasant. The owner was eager to sell them the biggest diamond he had in the store, but neither the stone nor the mount were acceptable. The second store was no better.

So Colette asked, "Why not get your bride a smaller piece of better quality and more discreet appearance?"

A little embarrassed, John replied, "The bigger the better. My fiancée would be offended if I gave her anything under two karats. My parents would be humiliated, and I would be the laughingstock of the Asian community."

Colette looked at him and said, "Well, then, I will be no help to you because I like small, pretty, delicate things that are admired by me almost exclusively. I do not care what others think about my jewelry or my money. And I certainly don't want to be liked for what I have in my bank account."

John looked at her tenderly. This was one of the reasons he loved her so much.

He finally settled on a ring Colette would not have been caught dead wearing. It was ever so flashy. She could not understand how any woman in her right mind would want to see something like that on her finger every day for the rest of her life. But it was not hers, she would not be wearing it, and she had nothing to say about it. So she stayed quiet.

They walked back in silence to the car John had borrowed to drive to the city. Neither of them dared to speak. Now was not the right time to express their feelings. The repercussions would have been too great. Instead, John held Colette's hand in the same way a dying man would hold on to his beloved wife just before he passed on. He was holding on so tightly that he was hurting her. But Colette would not say anything. She welcomed the physical pain. She was hoping it would numb her heart. But it did not. She had promised she would not cry when this day came. And she would not. John deserved a wife who would get along with his family and who would give him the Asian children his parents expected. He deserved to be happy and proud of his family.

148

They were driving on the Bay Bridge, and Colette was attempting to lose herself in the view of the ocean below her. For once, the weather was nice, and it looked as if Tinkerbelle had been busy throwing pixie dust all over the bay. The ride home was almost magical. But the reality of the situation was overwhelming to both young people. Life was definitely not fair.

Soon John dropped Colette off at her house, and without even looking at her thanked her for being there for him. He had not walked out of the car and was avoiding any contact with her, for he knew that if he did either, he would never leave her. So he started the car again and drove off.

Colette was standing on the sidewalk. She had not cried, but she was completely numb. She had almost fainted when he left, and she could not breathe. Slowly, defeated by life, she walked to Rosie's to get George. She did not know how she was going to go on. Yet she knew she had to for her son's sake. She would probably throw herself into her work and would strive to make the best life she could for George.

After she had shared her misfortune with Rosie, her friend looked at her and said, "Colette, life has a way of working itself out. And it is generally for the best. When Mike died, I thought I had gone with him. But I survived and met Harold, who makes me extremely happy. I know you too will be happy someday. You just need to believe."

Colette smiled the sad little smile that one gives a friend who is trying to cheer you up but is ultimately failing. She hoped that Rosie was right, because right now her life seemed like a very long and lonely adventure.

As she walked home with George, she decided that she would go to bed early. George was generally in bed by eight o'clock, and she could not wait to follow his lead. She wanted this horrid day to end. Maybe tomorrow would be better, but today had really stunk.

***

It was just past midnight when she heard the doorbell ring. She had been asleep for a couple of hours and had a difficult time snapping out of it. But as the rings turned into impatient knocks, she finally got out of bed. She walked downstairs in her nightgown, and when she opened the door, she found John staring at her. He did not wait for her to invite him in.

He took her in his arms and started kissing her face, her eyes, her nose, and eventually her mouth with little pecking kisses as he told her, "I'm free,

Colette. I let her go. Marry me. Oh, please, marry me. I cannot live without you. I tried to tell myself that I could do right by my family, but I love you too much to be without you."

Colette was very confused. Not only was she half asleep, but her brain could not compute everything John was saying. So she asked him to take it from the beginning.

John replied, "I will tell you everything you need to know, but first promise me you will marry me."

In a daze, she promised.

For the next hour John described his trip to San José and how he had not been able to go through with the proposal. He had had a talk with his fiancée, who appeared as relieved as he was that the wedding would not take place. She was also in love with someone else and now had a chance at happiness too. She had wished John the best, and he had gone to her father to let him know that the wedding was off. Threats had ensued. And a lot of yelling…but in the end John left happy. He had made the right decision for both his ex-fiancée and himself.

Colette had listened to his story intently.

And after a moment of silence, she said, "The situation with your parents will not be easy. They might even disown you. Are you sure this is something you are willing to go through just for me?"

He was looking at her with such tenderness that the words did not really need to be spoken.

But nonetheless he said, "I just gave everything up for you, and I know I will never have any regrets. You make me want to be a better man. You bring out the best in me. You have had me, body and soul, since the day I almost ran you over by the trash cans. Granted it took me some time to find the courage to stand up to tradition, but now that I have found it, I will never go back."

Colette was beaming. "Body and soul, you say? I'd say that's a lie," Colette said with a little laugh. "I may have had your soul, but I never got your body. And I think it is time we changed that," she continued.

John did not need more encouragement. He took her in his arms and started kissing her wildly. He wanted to drink her in, to be one with her that instant. His hands were everywhere. He wanted to know her whole body right then and there. It was as if the universe wanted to have him make up for lost time in a single moment. But soon Colette stopped him.

He looked at her questioningly and blurted, "Not again!"

She laughed and replied, "No, but it would be nice if George did not find his mother sprawled naked on the sofa when he gets his nightly glass of water. I really think the bedroom would be more appropriate."

John blushed and had to agree with her, even though the mental image she had planted in his mind was more than appealing.

So they walked up the stairs and closed the door behind them. John very expertly and ever so gently removed the only piece of clothing that was covering her. She returned the favor and unwrapped her gift ever so slowly, until John was completely naked and as ready as he would ever be. She was surprised to see all the muscles of his chest and shoulders so clearly visible in the moonlight. He looked so strong and tight. She wanted to feel him under her fingers. And she was about to touch him when he stopped her hand in midair.

Gruffly, he said, "Please don't. I have wanted this for so long that I am already doing my best not to embarrass myself right this instant. If you touch me...that will be the end of that."

He then brought Colette to the bed and laid her down gently on the pillows. He caressed every inch of her body, studying her as he did, so he could observe her reaction, make sure she was comfortable with the intimacy, and eventually find the key to complete ecstasy. He waited patiently until she opened up for him. He wanted her to be in charge, to know that she could stop at any time. And when she was ready, she took his hand and placed it between her legs so he could alleviate the ache he had started there. When she came, John was almost brought to tears. She had trusted him enough to give him that gift. But she did not give him any time to ponder that thought too much.

In the heat of passion, she pulled him to her and said, "Now, John, now. I want you inside me now."

John could not stand it any longer and was more than happy to oblige. They looked at each other, lost in each other until they climaxed together at last.

John took Colette in his arms, and once again the feeling of well-being he sensed reinforced the idea that he had made the right choice.

She looked at him and said very simply, "Thank you, John. This was the first orgasm I ever had in my life that I did not have to give myself."

The young man did not know what to say. He was flattered but also felt sorrow for the life she had had to endure. He would make it up to her, he promised himself.

And without a moment's hesitation he said, "Does that mean I can stay?"

Colette was taken aback but soon remembered what she had told him weeks ago about the man she would agree to marry.

She smiled and replied, "You can stay…for now. But you need to keep up the good work."

And they both laughed.

CHAPTER 14

George walked into Colette's bedroom the next morning and found his mother and John talking. He did not seem surprised in the least to see them together there.

John took advantage of the fact that they were all present to solemnly ask the young boy. "George, I need to discuss something of great importance with you. You know I love you and your mother very much. I have known you since you were born, and I would like you and your mother to be a part of my family. What do you think?"

The boy looked confused, so John continued. "What I mean is…Would you please give me your authorization to marry your mother so we can all be a family and I can live with you all the time?"

George smiled and with a serious expression replied, "You have my authorization." And he jumped in John's arms and asked, "Can I have a piggyback ride now? I am hungry and would love some breakfast."

John indulged him, and they all walked downstairs.

As the little boy was having his café au lait and his toast, the groom-to-be addressed his bride. "I have to go see my parents to break the news. I will do it alone as I expect a major tantrum from both of them. Besides, I know you are going to run to Rosie's to give her the good news. I want to get married as soon as possible. But I thought we could have a civil wedding here within the next few months and then later on a religious blessing with your family in France. I have some money saved up, and I would love to be able to do that for you."

Colette was deeply touched by his thoughtfulness. She promptly agreed and said she would write to her parents soon to start arranging for the ceremony and party that would follow.

Without waiting another moment, John left to meet his parents. He knew Mr. and Mrs. Wu would not be pleased, but it had to be done, and John always did what he had to do. And as John had predicted, Colette ran to her friend's house to share the amazing developments that had transpired the night before. She told Rosie that she would have to plan on a trip to Europe because she was not getting married without her. Her friend was so happy for Colette that she laughed and even shed a tear or two, but she promised to be there no matter what. As soon as they were recovered from their initial influx of intense emotions, the two women started planning the American portion of the event, while Harold, who had stayed on the sidelines to watch cheerfully the announcement he had suspected for some time, took George by the hand and led him to the garden where he could help him mow the lawn.

***

John had barely pulled into the driveway when he saw his mother running toward him with a face as purple as an eggplant and eyes as red as the most scrumptious cherries tomatoes that could be found on this side of the Mississippi. This was not going to be fun. She had obviously heard from his ex-fiancée's parents and was about to have a coronary. He really hoped this was a figure of speech because she looked way too purple for her own good. But he had made his decision and would face the consequences, no matter how ugly they looked right now.

So he opened the car door as dispassionately as he possibly could under the circumstances and was welcomed by a strident voice screaming at him: "Are you trying to kill me? You ungrateful child! I gave you life, suffered for hours. You were a big baby, you know. And for what? To be betrayed, humiliated, ridiculed, deceived, disgraced, mocked by my own flesh and blood."

John replied with the imperturbability that can only be associated with James Bond and his British origins, "I see you have heard the great news. However, you have not heard it all. You are going to be so happy. You will have grandchildren. I can guarantee that because the woman I have chosen to marry already has one. So we know she can conceive. There is only one little glitch with my plan. She is white…and French. I hope you like the French. Well, probably not." And as his mother looked at him in shocked horror, he continued, "Oh, but don't worry, Mom, she did not have her son out of wedlock. She is divorced. There is a downside, however. She is an acupuncturist who has great respect for our traditions. But don't worry, she is not a pushover, and she will hold her own if she is attacked verbally or otherwise.

See? I knew she was the daughter-in-law you have always dreamed about."

John could barely control his urge to laugh. His mother was speechless, and that was extremely rare. Actually, he had never seen it happen before. He had always had a tense relationship with his mother. The old woman had tried to control him his whole life. She had even pretended to be dying when he was a child to make him behave the way she had wanted him to. He had been so scared. But not anymore. As he had envisioned, his beloved mother pretended to faint. Or maybe this time it was true. He was not quite sure.

So his father intervened and said, "John, you have had your fun. Now stop testing us, and tell us this was all a bad joke."

The young man just smiled and said, "No. It's all true, Dad. Her name is Colette, and she is really a wonderful woman. I have known her for a very long time and have been in love with her since we first met."

His father was angry and retorted, "But the whore was married. She should not have been involved with you."

John's temper was starting to flare. "She is anything but. And I would ask you to refer to my future wife with respect. You do not even know her, and yet you have already judged her. I expected bigotry from both of you but nothing like that. It is really amazing how you always manage to disappoint me no matter how much I try to prepare myself," the young man blurted out.

"Is that so?" Mr. Wu snapped. "You seem to forget, my child, who has fed you and kept you safe all these years."

At that moment John felt a hatred for his father he did not know he possessed. He responded, "You have had nothing but contempt for me since I was born. You have always preferred my brother and sister. I have been on my own since I was eighteen years of age and have not cost you a penny since. You are always so high and mighty, but take a look at your own life, your family, and their so-called happiness."

Indeed, the Wu family was a total disaster. John's sister Juliette was married to a rich man she hated and barely respected, while his brother Joseph was married to a Chinese woman who cheated on him left and right with every influential male in the Asian community. And his parents were not the picture of happiness either. They had always argued with each other and had been bitter individuals for the better part of their lives because of it. John wanted to make his own future with Colette. He knew she would make him happy. She already was making him happy.

Finally his father said, "Bring her over for dinner so we can meet her."

That statement chilled John to the bone. What did his father have in mind? He instinctively knew it could not be good.

And as he was leaving, his mother whispered in his ear, "I will never forgive her for having stolen my son from me."

Stoically, John answered, "I did not know you cared. Besides, you lost me a long time before she agreed to marry me."

***

When Colette raised her head, she saw John enter the store. He was as pale as he could possibly be. He looked as if he had fought the worst enemy in history. His jaws were locked tight, and so were his fists. She had never seen him that angry before.

So she asked with a touch of sarcasm, "It went that well?"

With a bitter smile, the young man replied, "Oh yes. But don't worry. They will come around. They have asked to meet you. It might be a good sign.

They want me to bring you over for dinner, and I think we should go."

Colette answered, "I agree. I think there is no point in hiding. I have gone against Nazi murderers. How much worse can this be?"

John did not say anything, but he thought to himself that the cuts his parents knew how to make could leave scars that were at least as deep if not deeper, because this time, it was personal. They were going after her because of who she was.

Rosie had witnessed the exchange between Colette and John. She was worried about the outcome of the future meeting and offered to watch George while Colette went to face her judge and jury. It would be best for him not to have to witness that. He was a happy child who lived in a happy environment, and it should be kept that way. John agreed with her assessment completely, and it did not take much for Colette to concur. She did not want to feel as if she was hiding her son because she was ashamed—she was not—but she wanted to protect him from whatever attack he might be the target of.

***

Colette and John were on their way to his parents' house for dinner. As planned, only the two of them would go, and they fully expected to have a dreadful war on their hands. They were holding hands in silence when they reached the front door. John rang the doorbell as any stranger would, and he waited for his mom to answer the door. When the old woman finally arrived, John held his breath. He knew his mother could be brutal. And even if Colette had been prepared, he knew that she would be in for a treat.

John's mother kissed him on the cheek and barely shook Colette's hand. But the real surprise was waiting for them when they entered the living room. There they found, sitting on the silk sofa, John's ex-girlfriend from high school, Lily. She was this petite Chinese girl, beautiful and gracious, who would not say a word until spoken to. John had liked her very much until he realized she had the makings of a great doormat. Everything he wanted she did for him. She would sit by him for hours while he read and not even make an attempt at simple conversation.

Lily quickly noticed that John was not so pleased to see her. She said, "Hello, John. Your mother invited me over for dinner. She said that you had been meaning to call on me for some time now, but that you did not know how to break the ice after your last letter to me. Maybe I should go now."

Mrs. Wu interjected, "Nonsense! John has been looking forward to reconnecting with you for some time."

The young man, who was not looking to hurt anyone, replied, "I would be happy to be friends with you. Let me introduce you to my fiancée, Colette. We are getting married in a few weeks, and I am very glad you two are meeting each other."

Lily opened her eyes as wide as she could in an attempt to prevent the tears that threatened to escape from reaching their goal. But she said nothing. She would never dare.

So Colette took over and said, "I am very happy to meet you, Lily. I do hope we will get to be friends. I should thank my future mother-in-law for her kindness in arranging this meeting. You and I should have tea soon. In the meantime we will enjoy this great reunion."

John's mother was fuming. She had expected this unanticipated meeting would cause a scene. But unfortunately it had not. So she started speaking Mandarin to Lily and John, leaving Colette out of the conversation. John promptly translated and asked his mother to speak in English. But she continued in her own language and was promptly joined by her husband.

John let the charade go on for a little while longer and then asked in English, "Why are you doing this? It is extremely impolite."

Colette squeezed his arm in an attempt to stop him.

But Mrs. Wu replied in Chinese, "We do this so your whore will not understand. She is not part of this family and never will be. We were hoping she would be at least smart enough to understand that on her own after she saw you with us."

John replied in English, "You know very well how I feel about this kind of language when it comes to my bride. Colette will be my wife in a few weeks. Please consider yourself uninvited to the wedding."

He turned around, took Colette by the hand, and pulled her out of his parents' house.

"Let's go eat at a restaurant where the people are friendly and the food is not poisoned," he said.

Colette smiled and replied, "As you wish…Your mom must have been really mean to you for you to leave the way you did."

He looked at her and said, "No. She was mean to you. She was trying to hurt you, and I will never let that happen. I love you too much for that.

My mother is evil. She does not care who she hurts as long as her purpose is served."

The next morning, as Colette was leaving her house to go to her first patient, she was accosted by her future father-in-law. His eyes were throwing daggers at her. She got the feeling that he was not here to bring her flowers and welcome her into the family. And she was not disappointed.

He looked at her straight in the eyes and said, "You are after my son's money, so I will give you what you want. Here is ten thousand dollars. Take it and disappear. I never want to see you again. Leave my son alone."

Colette was shocked that the man had the audacity to try to buy her, but she nonetheless replied, "You, sir, are despicable. I have no intention of taking your money or, for that matter, your son's. I am obviously not who you appear to think I am. But I will return the favor. I will expect you to start the most impressive disappearing act and never show your face at my doorstep again. That being said, I will not be as offensive as you, and I will thus not demean you by offering you money."

Mr. Wu left, obviously disgruntled.

As Colette was recovering from the shock she had suffered, John walked out of the house and placed himself right behind her. He put his arms around her and whispered, "I am so sorry. I had no idea they would go this far. I will go talk to them and make sure this will never happen again."

Colette turned around and said, "John, as much as you would like to, you will not be able to protect me all the time. I know they will try to get to me again, and that's okay. I can hold my own…You do know that nothing can change the way I feel about you. And I do appreciate the fact that you always want to defend me. But please don't say anything to your parents that you will regret. No matter what, they will always be your parents. Besides, they will come around."

CHAPTER 15

John and Colette had opted for a very small wedding at the local county clerk-recorder's office. Only George, Rosie, and Harold were present, and the ceremony was performed by the attending judge. John had steered clear of his parents and siblings so that they would not know the exact date and time of the event. Collette and John had made this choice in order to avoid having any unsightly scene on their wedding day. John's family had made it very clear that they vehemently opposed the event, and the groom wanted to be sure that this day would be perfect for his bride. So it was natural that the important date had been kept quiet.

The actual ritual was quick. The judge was a kind-looking man in his late fifties who thoroughly enjoyed marrying people. And as the weather was gorgeous, he offered to have the marriage ceremony outside by a nearby fountain. John and Colette were quite happy with this turn of events. The whole group gathered around the judge, who said a few words about the sanctity of marriage before he asked the questions everyone was waiting for. Finally both bride and groom said, "I do." And they were pronounced husband and wife.

John kissed Colette ever so gently. He had been dreaming of this moment for a very long time. And to think that he had almost married someone else, just to please his parents. It really was ludicrous, when he thought about it. But now Colette would be his forever. He would be able to wake up with her, fall asleep with her, protect her, cajole her, love her. He would not let anything bad happen to her, or George, for that matter.

Soon he was pulled out of his reverie. The judge was ready to congratulate them and go. John shook the man's hand, hugged his friends, and took George in his arms. The little boy was his son now. John's family was complete. He opted to carry George back to the car, as Colette held his other hand and as Rosie and Harold walked right behind them, smiling.

They first went back to John and Colette's place for some well-deserved champagne and appetizers that the bride had prepared before the wedding. Harold toasted the newlyweds, wishing them as much happiness in their marriage as he had in his. This, of course, earned him a big kiss from his wife, who could only agree with him wholeheartedly. And since John and Colette would be married in France in a religious ceremony the following year, the bride's family was not missed too much, and the groom's was not missed at all.

The group finally headed to the restaurant where John had made reservations. There was no way Colette was cooking for her own wedding, even though everyone knew that the food would most likely have been better. He had chosen to celebrate the day at John's Grill on Ellis Street in San Francisco. The place was known for its amazing steaks and heavenly seafood. Because of the quality of the establishment, John knew that everyone would find something they liked.

They were seated on the third floor at one of the corner tables. The room was a lot less crowded than the other two below, and the atmosphere was elegant and cozy. It was the perfect choice for a small wedding celebration. But in spite of all the choices that were available to them for their meal, John and his guests all opted for the prawn cocktail with sauvignon blanc, followed by the filet mignon with some pinot noir and then a slice of New York–style cheesecake with Dom Perignon champagne. John had called ahead to make sure they were brought a whole cheesecake that had been decorated with a little bride, groom, and small boy right in the center. It was not the big wedding cake everyone was used to, but it was his little gift to Colette until they could have the big wedding in France.

And John got the reaction he had hoped for. When Colette saw the cake arrive, her eyes filled with tears of joy.

She looked at her husband and whispered, "You really do think of everything. Thank you for this wonderful day, and thank you for marrying us." She wiped the moisture off her eyes and continued, "All good things come to those who wait. I waited, and here you are."

Sated, happy, and a little tipsy, they all decided to go for a walk and window shop until they felt their digestion was well under way. And as they left the restaurant, both staff and patrons who had seen the cake arrive wished them the best of luck and happiness as they embarked on this new adventure. After a good half hour of fresh air, George was getting sleepy, so John carried him for the last part of their stroll. And as soon as they entered the car, the child was fast asleep, a smile on his face. John loved this child. He had known him since he was born and could not imagine loving another child as much as him.

It was always a treat for Colette to cross the Bay Bridge and look at the city at night. But tonight was particularly beautiful. The air was warm in spite of the late hour, and the moon was out. The water looked as if little seeds of silver had been sown on its surface to provide the bride with a picture she would always remember. The city in the background was all lit up, and the buildings reminded Colette of her childhood Christmas trees. It was the perfect end to the perfect day. In spite of her family's absence, John had managed to make it a day they would always cherish. And it was more than enough to wait until they were ready to go to France for the wedding she had always dreamed of.

As they approached the house, John noticed his parents' car parked right across from his home. And since no one in his family had been apprised as to when the event was going to take place, it was only logical to conclude that his parents had had him followed. John was not pleased. He had planned on inviting Rosie and Harold in for a nightcap, but he would drop them off at their house instead. He would then get George and Colette into the house from the back and would go meet his parents outside alone to see what they had to say that could not wait until the next day. He told his new wife of his plan and went for it. Once George was tucked in bed, he asked Colette to wait for him in their bedroom. He would be up as soon as he could. And then he went to brave the storm.

John's parents walked out of the car as soon as they saw him. It had been a very long time since he had seen his parents do anything together. In fact, he could not remember ever seeing them agreeing on anything. They must have thought this situation required a perfectly united front. John laughed at the idea that it took such a deep hatred of his wife to see them join forces. He would hear them out, but he had no doubt that the outcome of this impromptu meeting would not be a pleasant one.

And once they were close enough to be heard without yelling, his father said, "You know son, it is not too late. We know that you got married today, but you can get an annulment tomorrow...or even next month...I do understand how you can be attracted to a woman like your Colette, but you did not need to marry her. She would have had sex with you anyway."

The more his father spoke, the more John wanted to vomit. He could not believe such vile words could come out of the man who had raised him, who had made him the man he was today.

Finally he said, "You don't get it, do you. I love my wife, and I intend to stay married to her until the day I die. You have judged her without even knowing her. To you the fact that she makes me happy, that she challenges me, and that she makes me a better man is unimportant. You would want me to be as miserable as you have been, as long as I kept up appearances for your friends and associates. Well, it is not going to happen. Good night."

John had started walking back toward the house when he heard his mother say, "We will never accept her. And any child that comes out of her will never be our grandchild. Know this, John: you will never be able to bring your children to our home. They will never have grandparents. You are no longer our son."

The young man turned around and replied, "I am truly sorry you feel that way. But let it be known that she has never asked me to choose between you and her. You have. And sadly, the choice is made. She is my wife, my family. Good-bye."

And he closed the door behind him. He did not even wait to hear the car start. He went upstairs to his wife and hugged her in the way a drowning man holds on to a life preserver until the tears started flowing. She did not ask what had happened. She let him cry as she stroked his head and back. She looked up and offered her lips to him in the gentlest way she knew. And because she could do nothing else to make him feel better, she made love to him until he was too tired to stay awake.

She had never imagined her first night as Mrs. Wu would be such a bittersweet affair. But he had been the faithful man she had always known him to be. And when he had been forced to choose, he had chosen her. Her and her son. They were a family, all three of them, and no one would ever change that. She could hear John breathe peacefully next to her. In his sleep, he reached for her hand. And for a long time, she let him hold it, enjoying the feel and warmth of him. When she was done pondering the way her life had turned out, she finally went to sleep too.

CHAPTER 16

All had been quiet on the western front for the last few weeks. John and Colette were enjoying married life and the immense satisfaction of not having to say good-bye in the evening. They would fall asleep in each other's arms after talking, laughing, and making love into all hours of the night. John would take George to school every morning as Colette got ready to go see patients. John would then go to work in the new car they had just bought. He had found a job as a civil engineer in an architect's firm he had interned with before the war. He was responsible for reviewing the structural integrity of the buildings his boss was designing. He loved his job almost as much as he loved his wife, he thought one day as he entered his office. Life was good. And tonight he would surprise his wife by coming home earlier. That would give him some time to play with George before the little boy had to go to bed.

***

Colette had been working diligently on patients all afternoon at the store. She generally did her rounds in the morning and worked in her clinic in the afternoon. She had just finished seeing her last patient when a chill went down her spine. At the same time, she thought of George. Something was going to happen to him. She could feel it. She started running toward the school. She had ignored her sixth sense once before, and it had cost a man his life. She was not about to do it again. In a few minutes, George would be out of school and walking home. She had to get to him before that. She knew it in her gut. Just a few more yards. She could make it. George was exiting the school when she saw two men grabbing his little arms.

She screamed as loudly as she could, "Germans! They are trying to kidnap my son. Stop them!"

The adults started to look around for the offenders, who had just stopped in their tracks.

By then, George was also screaming, "Mom, don't let them take me!"

And with a speed Colette did not know she possessed, she closed the gap that separated her from her son. And as John had taught her, she landed the hardest roundhouse kick she could deliver to the kidneys of one of her son's assailants. The man screamed in pain and dropped to the ground, unable to move. The other was about to take off with George when the little boy kicked him in the chin and elbowed him in the groin. At the same time, Colette hit the back of his head with her arm, as both mother and child screamed, "Kiai!" The second man joined his friend on the ground, unconscious.

Colette moved back to the first man she had kicked and asked, "Who are you, and what do you want with my son?"

The man whispered in a strong German accent, "How did you know we were German?"

Colette heard a pop.

The German then said, "They will never leave you alone. They will not rest until you and your son are dead."

"Who are 'they'?" Colette asked as she saw foam coming out of his mouth. "Shit, the idiot has popped a cyanide pill," she said as she watched him take his last breath.

She needed to keep the other man alive so she could interrogate him. But first she had to move him before the police got here, because once they got him, she would not have the chance to talk to him again. But the second she formulated the thought, a police car arrived at the scene.

In the background she could see John running toward them. She was holding her son close to her as she answered questions the investigator was throwing at her.

John finally caught up with them and asked, "What is going on, officer? I am this woman's husband. Colette, George, are you okay?"

The young man was obviously very concerned, especially after he saw a body bag on the ground and an ambulance arriving.

The policeman replied, "Your wife is a bona fide hero. She single-handedly dropped the first of your son's assailants and helped this young man finish off the second."

George's chest puffed right up. He was so proud of having been called a young man.

"What do they want with my family?" asked John.

"That we don't know. The first one committed suicide, and the second is not talking yet," replied the officer. "But we will let you know as soon as we find anything out."

Frazzled, George and his parents walked home. Colette explained to John what had happened in great detail and recounted what the German had said just before he died.

Colette continued, "I don't understand. The war is over. Besides, I killed one man, not a whole army. There must be more to it than that. I am going to need to talk to the prisoner in order to figure out where that threat is coming from. The dying guy was very adamant that whoever had started this was not going to stop until George and I are dead."

John was very glad he had been teaching Colette and George how to defend themselves. They had been lucky this time. They had had the element of surprise. And thank God for Colette's woman's intuition. They could have lost George forever. John knew without a doubt that losing the little boy would have killed his wife. He needed to be even more vigilant. Tomorrow he would hire a private investigator to keep an eye on them and protect them should anything like that ever happen again.

***

Colette had asked on numerous occasions to be given the opportunity to talk to the prisoner. And every time she was given the runaround, then was handed a big fat no, and was finally promised that an explanation would follow. She was tired of waiting. Her son was not safe. It was time to call in some favors and use her connections. She knew that one of the judges in Berkeley was a Freemason. She would contact him first. She did not even make an appointment. She went straight to his office and waited for him to get out of court. Rosie would pick George up from school, so she had plenty of time.

When the man finally came out, she asked him if she could have a moment of his time; and as she spoke, she shook his hand and gave him the signal. She was immediately ushered into the judge's chambers. She introduced herself and explained her predicament.

"I would not be bothering you with this if I had any other option. And I do apologize for any inconvenience this may cause you," Colette said.

The judge replied, "No inconvenience. Go home. One of our brothers will contact you tomorrow and will take you to see the prisoner. You will have time to ask him all the questions you need."

The next day a young police officer arrived at her door and took her to the jail. The German was waiting for her in an interrogation room, all smug and obviously not willing to cooperate.

She asked him questions, and to each he just replied, "You are going to die, bitch. And so is your son. That will make my detention well worth it."

Colette had brought her travel kit with her as she always did. She opened it and placed the biggest, longest needle she could find on the table.

She looked at the German with a calm and icy expression. "You obviously knew the man I killed in France. But do you know how I killed him and how long I humiliated him before he died? I have as much time with you as I want, and I have all the equipment I need to make you talk and to kill you very…very…slowly, should I decide to do so. So it seems to be in your best interest to start making me your best friend."

The man had not been expecting that. This woman, in his opinion, had cost the Germans the war and his best friend his life. But she had been an amateur as far as he knew. She had done that only to save her brother and had never been involved in anything else after that. So how could she be so calm and collected?

Colette interrupted his reverie. "I will do anything to protect my son, even if it means using all my contacts' influence to get the US president to drop a nuclear bomb on the city where your wife and children live. I don't care about anything except saving my son's life."

"You're bluffing," the German replied.

"Maybe. But it took me about twelve hours to get to you once I started calling in favors. Are you ready and willing to call my bluff? It's a big gamble. But then again, maybe your wife and kids don't mean much to you. So when they die, you will not miss them much. Too bad, but I will settle for that," she said as she got up and started to put her needles away.

"You would not dare," the man said.

Anger and hatred blazing in her eyes, Colette replied, "Try me, if you feel lucky!"

She was about to walk out the door when the man stopped her. "Okay, ask away," he said. "I may not have all the answers, but I will tell you what I know."

"Who sent you, and why?" she asked.

"There is an underground group of Nazi resistance that is hunting all the war criminals, all the people that have contributed to the downfall of our great empire. We find these criminals, and we kill them and their offspring, just to make sure there will be no retaliation. As to why we are after you…you already know the answer to that," the man answered.

Colette continued, "How did you find me?"

"We were contacted by a man who knew of your whereabouts and wanted you eliminated as much as we did, if not more," he responded.

"Who was this man?" Colette wanted to know.

"I only know he is American. And he knows a lot about you and your habits," he said.

Then she asked, "Have you ever met him, and if yes, where?"

His answer was to the point. "Yes. Once in Chinatown, in San Francisco. And I will spare you the effort of having to ask the last question you want an answer to. He was wearing a hat but showed a little bit of blond hair. He had blue eyes. He was tall, about six feet and four inches, with very broad shoulders.

And no, I do not have a name. And if I did, it probably would not be his real one. Will that be it, or do you have other questions that need answers?"

Colette left and walked back home. She did not feel like taking a taxi. She needed the time to think and sort out all that she had learned during the day. The description she had gotten of the man who had sold her to the Germans fit that of her ex-husband. But why would he want her and George and her dead? He was arrogant and did not like to be reminded of prior mistakes. But would that be enough to want them eliminated? Something told her that she was barking up the wrong tree.

When John got home, she started recounting the conversation she had had with the prisoner.

"How did you manage that?" John asked, surprised.

"There is one thing I have not told you about me that I need to share with you right now. I am a Freemason. As such I have a lot of brothers and sisters around the world who are ready to help me when I need them. This was one of those times," she answered before she continued with the detailed account of her day.

John thought he had married the niftiest woman on earth. His wife was a shaker and a mover.

Well, no. But she had access to shakers and movers. And that was awesome. But he needed to concentrate on the task at hand. Something Colette had said had triggered an alarm. Like her, he did not think that Adam had anything to do with this, even if he fit the description of the man who had talked to the German. What was more interesting to John was that a group of white people had decided to meet in Chinatown. That was not the way to be the most inconspicuous. He would have to contact the private investigator he had hired to run it by him and get his thoughts on the matter. Something was definitely fishy. But he stayed quiet and for once did not share his thoughts with Colette. He wanted to be sure before he said anything.

***

William Blake, the PI John had hired, arrived a few minutes early for his appointment with his employer. They had met a few days prior and had discussed what had transpired regarding the secret meeting in Chinatown. John, who had been eagerly awaiting his arrival, escorted him back to his office, where both men sat down. Blake seemed uncomfortable.

He finally stated, "John, what I have to say is not something that you will want to hear. I have checked and double-checked my facts, and there is no doubt. Adam Walker is not involved. He is still in Europe and has been there since the war ended with the exception of a few trips to Washington, DC. The man who met with the Germans actually works for your mother."

John did not know what to say. He could not believe it. He knew his mother was a mean, self-serving individual who only cared about her life and what she wanted, but he had never thought of her as a killer. And if William Blake was right, that was exactly what she was. He would have to confront her and figure out what she was up to. There was no way that his mother could have ordered his wife and child murdered. John was deeply troubled as he tried to persuade himself of his mother's innocence. At this point he did not think he could deal with any other outcome. It would just be too vile, even for the woman who gave him life.

CHAPTER 17

It was getting late. The wind had picked up, and the fog had come in. William Blake was cold. The walk from his car to his flat seemed to take forever. Maybe he was coming down with something. He would have to ask his client's wife for some herbs tomorrow. He had heard that she was very good at her job and was helping a lot of people every day. He heard a noise and turned around. But the street was dark, and he could not see anything. He pulled his coat closer to him and lifted the collar as high as he could. Just a few more yards, and he would be home. He finally got a glimpse of the light that glowed in the stairwell of his apartment building. And that was all he ever saw. He felt a sharp pain at the base of his skull as the blade severed his spinal cord. There was no screaming, no fighting, just a little swoosh as his assailant helped him ever so gently to the ground.

***

John stopped the car in front of his childhood home. He could not believe what he was about to do. But it had to be done…He rang the front door and waited anxiously for someone to answer. He had started pacing nervously, wondering if his parents would let him in, when finally one of the servants opened the door. John smiled and said, "Is my mother home? I would like to speak to her." The woman who had let him in would not even look at him. This was not a good sign. But she nevertheless showed him to the study, where he found his mother sitting at her desk.

"Your father and I have been expecting you," she said.

Was this an admission of guilt already? John would not be so lucky.

So he replied, "Hello, Mother. And why is that?"

She retorted, "Don't play dumb with me, child. It does not suit you. Say what is on your mind now, or get out."

"I see that the last few weeks have not made you any sweeter, Mother. But that being said, I am here to ensure my family's safety. I know you had a hand in the attack on George that occurred a couple of weeks ago. I want to know why, and I want you to stop," John calmly answered.

"What makes you think I had anything to do with it?" the older woman continued.

"I hired a PI who put two and two together after Colette interrogated the remaining German. He has a case against you that he intends to give me for protection. I can do with it as I please," John commented.

His mother laughed and answered ever so sweetly, "Are you threatening me, my dear boy? You should first know that your PI is dead. So he will not be doing me much harm."

John was stunned. He did not know the woman who was standing in front of him. His mother had never been very loving, but he had never thought she was insane and bloodthirsty.

Shaken by this revelation, he asked, "You had him killed?"

His mother, now very annoyed, replied, "Of course I had him killed. I could not allow him to provide you with the file that would be my doom. Now you have no proof, so I am safe. As for your little wife and her son…well…they need to leave. You see, it is very simple. She steals my son, and I steal hers. That's the way life works. She has twenty-four hours to disappear, or I will have them hunted down and killed. And don't think for a minute that you will be able to protect them."

John had what he needed, but he wanted to clarify one last point, so he asked, "Was Father involved in any of this?"

His mother laughed yet again—the creepy guttural laugh of a villain on a radio show—and said, "Of course not. Your father does not have the guts for this kind of stuff. He has a loud bark, but I run the show. As a matter of fact, I think he would be a little shocked to find out I had tried to have them removed in such a fashion."

John had had enough.

And in his most commanding voice, he said, "Officers, you can come out. And so can you, Father."

Two officers entered the room and said, "We heard it all. Thank you. Now we will bring her in and charge her with murder and two counts of attempted murder."

His father was now standing in a corner of the room, his eyes misting and a strange smile on his face. He was shaking his head. He was obviously in shock.

He looked at his wife as she was being handcuffed and asked, "Is that really what you think of me? All I am guilty of was trying to make you happy. Yes we fought all the time, but I was always very sure that we loved each other."

The older woman laughed. "You are so gullible. I married you because I knew I could control you. You were so goo-goo eyed all the time. It was just too easy to manipulate you."

She really was a mean individual and had always been. Even the officers looked at her with disgust.

The old man then turned to his son and said, "You should not have done that. She is family, and family comes first."

"Is that why you stayed with her for so long, Father? Because she is family?" John answered.

"I love your mother," Mr. Wu retorted. He continued, "It was having children that destroyed our lives. But she wanted to have some, so I went along with it. As with everything she wanted…"

John looked at him, puzzled. He could not believe what was coming out of his father's mouth. He finally said, "I feel so loved right now. Thank you for all your support."

Enraged by what his son had just said, the old man snapped, "Oh, grow up already. Now I have to clean up your mess and get your mother out of jail."

And he stormed out before his son could say another word.

John was sad it had to come to this. No matter what, these people were his parents, and that would never change.

Before his mother was put in the police car, he asked to talk to her one last time. "Mother, how did you pull it off? How do you get people to do all your dirty work like that?"

The older woman smiled sadly and said, "I had such high hopes for you. I wanted you to become my second in command. I wanted you to take over when I retired. But instead you became an engineer. And now you sold me out to the police. If you had wanted to know more, you should have been more involved with your family. Now it's too late."

Then looking at the police officers, she continued, "Take me away. I am done here."

John stayed for a while after the police car had left. It was probably one of the most painful moments in his life. Because of his mother's actions, he had almost lost his wife and child…and he had lost a mother. Now he would have to go home and face his Colette. He would have to bear the shame of what his family had done, and he would have to admit it to his wife. He was afraid of her reaction. What if she blamed him? What if she thought he was like them? After all, he shared the same genetic makeup. He could have the same character traits. God, he hoped not. He knew he would never hurt his wife and child the way his parents had hurt him. Or any other way, if he could help it.

He also had to make sense of what his mother had said. They had always had a beautiful home. His family was well respected in Chinatown. He repeated this thought to himself and started wondering…Was it respect, or was it fear? He would have to investigate. His mother had obviously hired thugs and had also acted like one. The woman was something else. He was not sure he could deal with finding out that the members of his family were not the respectable business people he always had been led to think they were.

All this thinking had taken enough time to allow him to come back home. He parked his car in front of the house and walked inside. Colette was sitting on the floor by the fireplace, helping George with a new puzzle. They were halfway done and looking for a piece of the bridge that made up part of the picture. As usual, Colette looked lovely. John walked up to them and kissed them both on the cheeks.

He looked at the little boy and said, "George, would you mind finishing the puzzle with Mommy in a few minutes? I need to talk to her right now. It is rather urgent."

The little boy looked up and answered, "Sure thing. Can I go play in my room while you guys talk?"

John smiled and said, "Absolutely. If you want, I will call you when we are done."

And before John had finished his sentence, George had run up the stairs and gone into his room.

"I went to my parents today," John started to say as he looked at his inquiring wife.

He continued, "After you mentioned Chinatown as a meeting place, I became very suspicious. So I asked a PI to look into it, and after he gave me his verbal report involving my mother, he turned up dead."

All the blood had drained from Colette's face. She looked as if she were going to faint. John rushed to her and helped her sit on the sofa.

"She hates me this much…" the young woman whispered.

John was dying inside, but he had to finish telling Colette everything. It was the only way they would both be free of all this horror.

So he plowed on. "I knew I had to stop her. So I went to the police and devised a plan to have her confess in front of witnesses. Well…not quite in front."

The young woman was listening intently, giving John her undivided attention. She was going from shock to shock, but she wanted to hear what her husband had to say.

"I had the maid get my father and ask him to stay hidden by the door of the study while two police officers came from the back door and moved into position to be within hearing distance of my mother and still remain unseen. I then pushed her to confess everything to me," John explained.

"How did you get your father and the maid to cooperate?" interrupted Colette.

John answered, "Oh it was easy enough once they realized that if they did not, they would all go to jail. My father may be weak when it comes to my mother, but he is no fool. He knew that being on the outside was the best way to help her while she was in jail."

The young man went on to give her all the details of the conversation, including the one he had had with his father afterward.

Colette's heart was breaking. She was shocked that so much hatred could be present in a single family. She felt for John, who had suffered the consequences of betraying his mother in order to save George, and who had had to endure his father's admission that he had never wanted him. She looked up into her husband's eyes, and the pain she saw broke all the barriers that were keeping her from losing it. Then one tear fell. Then another. And there was nothing she could do to stop them. She had not spoken since John had finished his rendition of the past events. The young man took her in his arms and started rocking her. And in the process of appeasing her, the dam that had kept his own pain in check broke. John started sobbing like a little child. He could not believe he had been deceived by his own flesh and blood. He could not believe he had almost lost his wife and child because of his mother. He had promised himself to protect them, always. And instead, he—well, his family—had almost destroyed what he cherished most. How could his wife ever forgive him for such a failure?

Colette, who was somehow sensing some of what was going on in his mind, finally spoke. "I am so proud of you, John. You are the strongest man I know. I can only begin to imagine what you are going through. In spite of everything, you did the right thing, and you did not even waver from your path. I have such admiration for your courage. You have always been my hero. But today…That is something else. I love you so much. I love you for loving my son as if he were your own. I love you for all the laughter you bring into my life every day. I love you for the strength you send my way when I need it most. But most of all, I love you for being you. Don't ever change, my love."

John was moved to the core by the words his wife had just uttered. He knew Colette loved him, but until now, he had not realized how much. He had also not realized how fair she was. She was not blaming him. She was admiring him. As if it were possible, at this very moment he loved her even more.

CHAPTER 18

The Wu family had hired the best attorneys money could buy. The trial was supposed to last a couple of months. John was following the events from afar. He had hired a few Berkeley students to cover the trial during their time off and to give him daily reports. He had been relieved to find out his mother had not been allowed to post bail. He had been concerned about what she would try if she had been released during trial. He knew she could not be trusted. To his surprise, her defense had been based on an insanity plea. The prosecutor had not bought it and was moving forward with the trial. His mother would have an interesting time showing she was insane, he thought, even though he knew full well that she was.

John's father was standing by his mother, as he had said he would. He was at the courthouse every day, getting instructions from her and her team of lawyers. Now he would have to find psychiatrists that would be willing to say that his wife was insane. The elderly man looked much older than he had a few months ago. The stress of the situation was getting to him, and John almost felt sorry for him. But the young man would never forget his father's last words to him. He knew he could no longer trust his progenitor, because the old man would do whatever it took to get his wife out of jail, no matter how vile her behavior and words had been.

John only had one goal: keeping his family safe from the monsters his parents had become. So when he had been ask to be a witness for the prosecution he had agreed, though with a heavy heart. The days were as gray as his mood, but when the time came he did what was asked of him. He had not seen his parents in a few months and was surprised to see that the trial had not only affected his father but that it had also taken its toll on his mother. She looked much older and a lot less refined. She was not wearing any of the jewelry he was accustomed to see her show off. She was understated and looked like a little old lady who would want to bake cookies for her grandchildren and spend her days rocking and knitting in her chair. It was a far cry from the reality John had experienced, and after the initial shock of this unusual display, the young man realized it was all theatrics played out for the jury's benefit.

The prosecutor asked John to recount his story, and the young man obliged as efficiently as he could. The lead defense attorney, once given the opportunity to cross-examine, went for the jugular. Instead of discrediting John's story, he went after the young man himself. He brought up his childhood and his parents' reaction to his marriage to Colette. It was clear to John that this bully of an attorney was trying to anger him in order to prove this was a situation in which a son was just trying to pay his mother back for the harsh treatment he had suffered. The attorney was also trying to make it appear that John was fully responsible for his mother's temporary insanity. John, having had to deal with a very difficult mother his whole life, was used to these types of maneuvers. He remained stoic and answered the questions in a calm and intelligent manner. The DA was quite happy with John's performance. He had not fallen into the trap the defense had prepared for him, and thus he was hopeful that his mother would remain in jail.

***

In spite of her mother-in-law's trial, Colette was still preparing the upcoming religious wedding that would be performed in France that summer. John had insisted on it. His parents would obviously not be present, but his sister, Juliette, and her husband would be there to represent his family. So Colette had been writing furiously for the last few months. Eventually her parents would have to make the final decision as to where all the festivities would occur. She had been adamant that she wanted to get married in Brittany. She loved the area. Not only was it beautiful, but the energy there was also amazing. Whenever she visited the little village of Le Vivier sur Mer, she felt at peace. She had good memories there. And the church was so pretty. No, she would have it no other way. Paris was not an option, even if it were possible to be married at the Notre Dame cathedral. As for the food, she trusted her parents would make the best choice. They had enlisted her beloved godmother to help with the decision making. Her godmother was also her aunt and her mother's sister. Like Colette's grandmother, her godmother had played a pivotal role in the young woman's life. She would be very happy to see her again.

All she had to do here now was to take care of her wedding dress. She would bring it on the boat with her because she would have no time to have it made when she arrived in Paris. John had planned on having them arrive with George two weeks before the event. That way they could help with the final preparations. After the wedding, they would then take a few days away from George, who would stay with his grandparents so that Colette and he could enjoy a short honeymoon.

The young woman had hired the services of a local seamstress, Mrs. Smith, who was known for her golden fingers and keen eye for fashion. Not only could she duplicate any design that was brought to her, but she could also evaluate how the final product would look on her client. Those who had not listened to her had lived to regret it. But thankfully, Colette was one of these women who could wear just about anything she wanted and still look amazing. Mrs. Smith just knew Colette would be one of the most beautiful brides she had ever seen. She could not wait until the final fitting and really wished she could be at the wedding to see John's reaction to his beautiful bride.

***

They were just about a month away from the wedding when the jury was sent on its way to deliberate. The question that needed to be answered was multifold. Was the defendant guilty of murder, and if she was, was she insane or temporarily insane? And if she was not insane, was she guilty of first-degree murder and was she also guilty of attempted murder? The deliberations could take weeks. John really wished this could be settled before they all left for France. He did not have much contact with his siblings and thus did not really know how they felt. Only on one occasion had his sister mentioned that their mother had been unwell and mentally unstable for some time now. She had even wondered if this problem had not been there before they were even born.

John had shared with his sister what his father had said about having children.

The young woman had just laughed it off and said, "Dear John, our mother taught me well. I can wrap our father and my husband around my little finger and get anything out of them. So I am definitely not an inconvenience to them."

John was annoyed by the snide remark and retorted, "Really? Is that why your husband has more mistresses than every senator sitting on the United States' Senate combined?

His sister turned beet red, and replied, teeth clenched, "I see you can still take care of yourself. Maybe you did drive our mother insane. My husband is exactly where I want him to be. When he sleeps with other women, I do not have to do it. And since he repulses me, I do believe it is to my advantage to have him run around with other women."

"Why don't you get a divorce?" John asked. "Would that not be better than to live a lie?"

Juliette did not bother to reply. She just grabbed her purse and coat, walked out of the restaurant where they had just had lunch, hailed a cab, and disappeared. John sat there thinking that maybe he had pushed her too far. After all, she had nothing to do with their parents' issues. She was his sister. And even if he did not agree with her choices in life, she had the right to make her own decisions and live whatever way she pleased. Far from him the idea to become a bigot like his parents. He knew he had hurt her, and he regretted it.

***

John barely had a foot in the door when Colette told him that the jury had made a decision and that the judge had called everyone back in. Without hesitation he went back to his car and drove to the courthouse. He was anxious and worried. He had mixed feelings. He wanted his wife and child safe, but he also did not want his mother to die. And if she was convicted for first-degree murder, she might be sentenced to death.

When he walked in the door, his parents were already present, and so were his brother and sister. His siblings were sitting together, but John sensed that he would not be welcome sitting with them. He was seen as the traitor in his family. They did not even make eye contact with him. So he sat alone. He had insisted that Colette stay with George. He did not want her to have to face the whole clan under these circumstances.

The jury sat down, and the judge came in. The rest was just a big blur for John. His mother was being taken away and was glaring at him. This time she had made eye contact, and the look he saw coming his way chilled him to the bone. He let the whole room clear and went to find the bailiff to ask him to recap what had just happened.

The man, seeing the aggrieved look on John's face, obliged. "Well, she was found guilty and insane. She is going to be taken to the loony bin. The judge will decide tomorrow for how long and under what circumstances she might be allowed back into society. He will be hearing more witnesses. You may want to be there to testify again so he can keep her locked up for as long as she lives."

John was relieved and panicked at the same time. He would have to testify against his mother yet again. But she would not be put to death.

The next morning, John drove back to the courthouse. But this time, Colette was with him. She had decided that she would not let him face that ordeal alone again. After all she was not made of sugar. She could take it. She knew it was going to be hard, but she needed to be there for John.

They both sat down, hand in hand, and waited for John to be called to the stand. The judge saw Colette and smiled at her in a reassuring way. And to Colette's great surprise, he called her to the stand.

The young woman was sworn in, and the judge asked, "Mrs. Wu, can you please explain to me what happened the day your son what attacked and how your life has been affected since that day?"

Colette accommodated him and recounted everything that had happened. She then talked about the fear she felt every time her son had to leave her side. She always wanted to be near so she could get to him quickly if need be. She had not felt safe since the incident.

She was taken back to her seat, where she waited for all the witnesses to have their turn testifying. The judge finally called John's mother to the stand. The old woman was crying. She expressed her regrets. She looked at Colette and reaffirmed that she would never want to hurt her or her child again.

After all, she was family now. She could see how much John loved her and how much her daughter-in-law was making her son happy. She continued by telling the whole court how much she wished she could take everything back. Colette wanted to welcome the old woman into her life. She always knew Mrs. Wu would come around. It was just too bad it had to come after such an ordeal. If Colette could be on speaking terms with her, it would make John's life so much easier. Besides, she had been diagnosed with mental illness. How could anyone hold mental illness against another person? She would write to her tomorrow and start establishing relations. If she could help the old woman recover, she would. And even if she believed her mother-in-law might never got better, she was a healer, so it was her duty to try.

CHAPTER 19

Le Vivier sur Mer, July 1947

The trip had been a long one. They had taken the train from Oakland to New York with a few stops in between and had sailed from the Big Apple to Brest. The downtime they had had on the boat had been welcome. Not only did they have the opportunity to enjoy each other's company, but they were also able to give George their undivided attention to play the many board games he always enjoyed. And once they had landed, they had driven to the north of Brittany to meet up with Colette's family, which was already there for the final preparations. They would have two weeks before their wedding day, and that would be just enough time to apply the finishing touches to their matrimonial project.

The culture shock John experienced when they arrived at their destination was beyond anything he had anticipated. They had parked right on the beach in the parking lot of the Hotel de Bretagne, where they would be residing during their stay. The vacation rental that Colette's grandmother's had found for herself was on the side street that led to the beach. And since the old woman had been watching for them, she warned every one of their arrival within seconds. Who knew an elderly female could move so quickly? Family members and close friends were coming out of all the surrounding homes to welcome them to the village. And even though John had studied French for quite a few years now, he was overwhelmed with the speed at which they were all firing questions at him. At a loss for words, he looked at Colette, who was obviously right at home in this environment. She went around the car to be by his side, followed by some of the younger children she did not know yet.

Once she had his hand safely linked to hers, she quieted everyone down and announced in the most perfect French, "As you may have guessed, this is John, my husband. He does speak French, but do give him a few minutes to get used to the speed with which we are accustomed to communicate. Speaking slowly will get you a long way."

Then Colette went to her grandmother, who had been waiting in the background. The old woman kissed her granddaughter soundly on both cheeks and did the same to John. "Welcome to the family, my dear," she said to him. "You seem to be taking good care of my granddaughter and great-grandson, so you are okay with me. Call me Grandma," she concluded.

John smiled and replied, "Grandma it is, then."

He liked the old woman. She was friendly and honest. One could instantly tell that she would call it the way she saw it and that she did not mind ruffling a few feathers if that was going to better a situation.

Colette was already pulling John toward her parents. Again the kissing ceremony took place. Even the men kissed. "But just because they were from the same family," his wife had explained. Otherwise, men shook hands just like they did in the United States. His in-laws were Papa and Maman. Easy enough. He should be able to remember that. Then there was Colette's sister, Josette, with her husband. And again, the kissing. But when Colette reached Pierre, her brother, she hugged him fiercely. There was a bond between them that only they could understand. Pierre had been to hell, and Colette had gotten him back. Because of her bravery and selflessness, he was alive. He owed her his life, and he would never forget it.

She looked at his hands and said, "Well, you will never be a pianist, but they healed nicely."

"Always the doctor, I see," he said with a laugh. And then looking at John, he continued, "Welcome to the family. You keep doing right by her, you hear? She deserves it."

Pierre had spoken English with a combination of a French and a British accent, and acknowledging this, he commented, "I like speaking English when I can, so I don't lose it. I hope you do not mind the accent too much."

He wanted his brother-in-law to feel at home. He liked the man who was taking care of his sister and nephew.

John smiled and replied, "Pierre, you are a godsend. I do not mind one bit. As a matter of fact, I had not even noticed!"

Now both men laughed.

Colette walked into the kitchen of the small house her grandmother was living in for the summer. It was rather dark inside, but the young woman could make out the form of her dear friend Anne, who was rocking quietly in a chair. Richard was standing in a corner looking at her.

"She has barely said a word since the incident," he said.

"What incident?" asked Colette as she was walking to her friend.

She grabbed the other woman's hand and said ever so gently, "Tell me, Anne. Tell me what troubles you."

Anne looked up and smiled the sad little smile of people who have seen and experienced too much.

"You came back! I am so glad you did. I missed you so much…" she said in a strange little voice Colette had never heard come out of her friend before. "They took the bicycle, you know, right after they killed the baby. Yes…the parents…they needed the bicycle to escape the bombs with their baby. And the two German soldiers…they told them to give them the bicycle…and when they refused and explained that they needed it for the baby, the Germans just shot the baby girl and took the bike, claiming that now the parents did not need it anymore."

Anne stayed quiet for a few very long seconds and continued with tears now rolling down her cheeks. "There was nothing I could do, Colette. I am not you. I do not have your strength."

"Oh, dear Anne, there was nothing anyone could have done, and least of all me," Colette exclaimed as she hugged her friend tightly. "What you saw was horrible, but the death of the baby was not your fault. You have to start living again, my dear; otherwise, we won the war for nothing. Those ugly Germans will have had their victory. They will have that power over you. And you cannot let that happen. Ever!"

As she finished her speech, Colette was shaking. She believed every word she had just told her friend. And she had to; otherwise, she would not have survived what had happened to her and what she had had to do to save her brother and herself.

And for the next hour, not caring that Richard was still looking at them, Colette shared with Anne what had happened the last time she came back to France. The two women cried in each other's arms and began their healing process at the same time. What had remained buried for so long in Colette and what had kept Anne from living her life came out in the open. It felt good not to hide anymore. It felt wonderful to acknowledge the terror and the shame. It felt right to be allowed to feel and grieve what had once been. And it felt particularly good to be angry and to share it with the world. These two women had been wronged and they had survived. They would not let circumstances beat them down.

Richard could not believe what was happening right in front of him. His wife was coming back to life. Ever so slowly, and by sharing her own weaknesses and nightmares, Colette was pulling Anne back up to the world of the living. He could see the emotional pain his cousin was going through. But he was so thankful for the outcome that he was not about to stop it.

Finally Colette said, "Tonight you will come out and have dinner with the rest of us. And we will dance. We will dance all night to celebrate our survival…and to honor those who have died so we could live. Will you do that for me, Anne? Will you do that for yourself?"

Anne got up and said, "You are right. Let me greet your new husband!" The young woman walked out and left Colette in the dark.

The bride-to-be was exhausted, but she stood up when she saw her cousin come to her.

"You did not have to do that," said Richard.

"Yes, I did," Colette replied. "I found out a long time ago that when you are ready to show your weaknesses to the world, the world is ready to do the same. It is a very therapeutic way of handling such a situation. Now Anne will be fine. And so will I. In fact, it was good for both of us."

Her cousin kissed her cheek and just said, "Thank you."

There was nothing more to say.

John had seen and heard everything from the door where he had been standing. It was when he saw his wife give so much of herself, and expecting nothing in return, that he admired her most. He was really marrying an exceptional woman. The young man had known about Colette's trip to France. She had told him once, and she had never spoken of it again. He knew her wartime experience had had a huge impact on her, but he had not fully comprehended the burden she was carrying until he saw her with Anne. She really was a wise woman. She was right. This had been good for her too.

John's sister arrived at the village the day before the wedding. The whole Wu clan had been invited, but only Juliette had decided to come. Colette's family had reserved a room for her at the local hotel where the bride and groom were staying themselves, in separate rooms, of course. True to the Wu tradition, all she could do was criticize everything in sight. The room was too small, and the bathroom was too far. The car that picked her up at the train station was too old. And French men were just too rude. None of the big men she had encountered had helped her with her large, heavy suitcases she was accustomed to travel with.

Dinner that night was going to be a lot of fun, Colette thought with amusement. John's sister was going to have to eat freshly picked and steamed mussels—the local claim to fame—and French fries, using only her fingers. Her sister-in-law always tried to look so proper, and yet she really was not. Colette would never tell John, but in France his sister looked more like a woman of the night than a proper Asian American lady. Too bad. It did not matter anyway. Colette's whole family was aware of what had happened with her in-laws in the United States, and if John's sister misbehaved, they would not hold it against John.

**

The evening had indeed been a lot of fun. After John had returned his sister to the hotel so she could get her beauty rest for the next day, the remainder of the guests started to sing and dance. They had had some good food and amazing wine. Everyone was happy, and the atmosphere was relaxed and congenial. John invited Colette to dance to a song he had never heard before, and he scored some points with the crowd when he brought Colette close to him, held her tightly, and then kissed her right on the lips. He wanted her. He wanted her now and forever. As a matter of fact, they would make their escape soon and go back to Colette's hotel room where they could enjoy each other's company, alone. But as they were about to leave, Anne and Richard stopped them along with Colette's father.

The old man said, "I want to be sure my little girl spends her last night alone. That will make tomorrow just that much more special. Besides it's bad luck and form for bride and groom to share the same bed the night before their wedding. Even if they were married in front of a judge and have shared the same house for a year. Anne will stay with Colette, and Richard will sleep with you John. Good night, everyone."

John looked at Colette expecting her to say something, anything.

But instead she looked at him and said with a beaming smile on her lips, "How romantic! That is a great idea. And this way, I get to talk to my dearest and oldest friend until dawn."

John could not help but return her smile. It was not what he had had in mind, but he would play along. They had their whole life ahead of them. And this way, he would get to know Richard a lot better.

The men decided to have a nightcap when they got to the room. They talked about their respective jobs. They even talked about the war and what they had survived. If the girls could do it, so could they. And after a few hours of drinking and bonding, they opted to go to sleep. Tomorrow would be a long day. And they would have to get up early to dress and be in church by eleven o'clock.

The girls skipped the drinking and talked until late into the night. They too would have to get up early so Colette could get her hair and makeup done before it was time to go to church. Her mom would be taking care of George, who had been deserting his mother in order to spend more time with all his newly found cousins. France was a lot of fun for him. He was finding out for the first time what having an extended family was all about. And he loved it.

CHAPTER 20

Colette looked amazing. She had just put on her wedding gown, and it fit her perfectly. Her hair had been made up into a bun, and the talented hairdresser had let escape little tendrils all around her face. Small white and orange flowers had been placed here and there in her hair. Her dress was a strapless number that hugged all the right places and ended in a beautiful train. Colette had opted not to have too much girly embroidery on it and to limit her jewelry to the moon pendant her mother had sent her and the pearl earrings John had given her the previous Christmas. With her godmother's help, she put on her veil, and she was ready to go. As custom dictated, she would walk into the church with her father, but John would enter with his sister.

When Colette made her entrance, John was waiting for her by the priest. She took his breath away. She was absolutely spectacular. Mrs. Smith had done an amazing job and had been right all along. The bride finally joined him at the altar, and her father lifted the veil to give her a kiss before he gave her hand to John. Colette's mother was crying softly, and her grandmother was keeping a handkerchief close by. Pierre was standing by his sister, as he had been asked to be her witness. John's sister would be his.

The ceremony was short and sweet. The priest blessed the rings and their union. They were asked to repeat the traditional vows, and John was finally allowed to kiss his bride. They were now husband and wife. The priest had said so. And as much as John had enjoyed spending the night with Richard, who was for all intents and purposes a very nice guy, John would be spending this night with his wife. She was much more pleasant to look at and snored a lot less.

When they exited the church, the traditional picture was taken with all the guests who were attending. For lunch, they all followed the young couple to the restaurant, where a five-course meal was served in honor of the newlyweds. Colette's family had gone all out. They had refused John's help in paying for their daughter's wedding. They wanted to do that much for the couple. As is the case with all wedding receptions, John and Colette spent more time standing and talking to guests than actually relaxing at their table. They would eat what was served in a hurry and do the rounds so they could talk to all the guests and thank them for coming. One of John's old roommates had made the trip to support the groom in his moment of need. The young American was thoroughly enjoying himself and getting more than enough attention from Colette's younger cousins. He was a charming lad whom Colette had known and liked for years. She was not surprised that he was such a hit with the female community of the family.

The party then moved to the village's recreation room for dinner, where a caterer was already preparing the dinner. Only a brief break had been taken so people could change into their evening attires if they wished to do so. A very talented one-man orchestra was to be the entertainment for the night. He had come highly recommended by a close family friend who had used him for her own wedding the year before. Again there would be singing and much laughing throughout the night. And of course there would be dancing—a lot of it.

John waited for a moment alone with his bride and took her away to the beach. The recreation room was right across from it, and he knew they could make a quick getaway before they would be really missed. The sun was setting, and the kids from their wedding party were playing in the sand. They had all traded their Sunday best for more comfortable and less expensive pieces of clothing that they could get dirty without getting into trouble. They spotted George. And as the little boy ran by them, they called out to him.

Not even stopping to talk to his parents, he said, "Sorry, Mom. I really don't have time to chat right now. But I promise to tell you all about my trip to France when we go home. Have fun, you two," he yelled as moved away.

The newlyweds laughed and looked at their son one more time before they walked back in.

The minute they returned, they were assailed by requests. And as tradition dictated, the bride and groom had to start the first dance. The whole assembly was waiting to dance, and they were more than happy to join in as Colette switched partners. It was a long time before John saw his bride again. The poor man danced with so many women that were not his. He really wanted to be with her again. But as usual, he was a good sport. After all, as he kept reminding himself during this trip, he had his whole life ahead of him. He danced with the women and drank with the men. The French in Brittany certainly knew how to throw a wedding party.

At the end of dinner, the guests were asked to sit down again, and the bride and groom were surprised by what they were served for dessert. Indeed, Colette's parents had ordered a replica of the church where they had just been married. The masterpiece had been made of cream puffs and nougatine exclusively. The whole crowd was in awe of the beautiful and original cake that was being served. It was a culinary masterpiece that deserved a picture before it was dismantled and eaten. John and Colette were supposed to cut the first slice. But the question was, how does one slice such a cake? Again John thanked God for his wife's resourcefulness. There was no way of cutting this thing, and everyone knew it.

So Colette went to the kitchen and then came back, saying to the audience, "My hands are clean."

She then proceeded to grab the top of the edible church with both hands so she could get to the first cream puffs. And when they were free to be picked, she removed three from the top. She placed them on a plate, and gave the offering to John.

She now looked at her family and said, "See, when you put your heart into it, and also your hands, it is really easy to cut. Wash your hands and enjoy!"

And having finished this short impromptu speech, she left the side of the cake. Everyone laughed. And the caterer, with much more class, and no hands, served all the other guests very artfully. And once the chef d'oeuvre was consumed, the dancing resumed.

Before anyone knew it, it was four o'clock in the morning and time to eat the traditional onion soup. The one-man orchestra had been a hit, and everyone had enjoyed the evening tremendously. John, who had been keeping an eye on his sister all night, noticed that even she had been smiling and dancing. She had come alone, as her cheating husband could not be bothered. And in spite of everything, Colette's family had made her feel welcome. The women had tried to talk to her using the minimal English that they possessed, and the men, being French, flirted with her and made her dance all night. She definitely had had a good time.

John was exhausted and ready for a nap. As a matter of fact, he suspected that all this eating and drinking was a ploy used by his in-laws to make sure he would not be enjoying his wife too much tonight either. John smiled. He was having the time of his life and was grateful for all the time and energy that had been put into preparing for this day. Not one person present would ever forget it, and he least of all. So when the bowl of soup was served, he picked up his spoon and ate the hot cheesy broth in which little croutons and caramelized onions were floating.

Finally the newlyweds were allowed to leave as the party continued.

They went back to their hotel, and as they closed the door to the room that was reserved for their wedding night, Colette said, "John, let's hurry up and get a couple of hours of sleep. They will be here to wake us up around eight this morning."

John could not believe his ears. They would be here when? And to what? Colette explained that it was tradition. They could either be in bed when the guests arrived, or they could set their alarm clock and surprise them by being up and having coffee by the window. It was a silly tradition, she agreed, and that is why she did not want to give them the satisfaction of being sound asleep when the guests got here. So they set the alarm and hopped into bed, hoping they would be able to fall asleep quickly.

As expected, the door to the bride and groom's door opened at eight o'clock sharp. Colette and John were sitting by the window having coffee and croissants for breakfast. Not expecting such a proper sight, everyone roared with laughter when they discovered their prey all dressed and completely awake. Colette and John thanked everyone for coming, kissed them all good-bye, and agreed to meet everyone at the village recreation room for lunch. They had planned on finishing the leftovers together there before they cleaned up the place and returned the keys to the mayor.

***

Since John's sister was leaving for Paris that afternoon, they were relieved from kitchen duty so that they could accompany her to the train station. She had checked out of her hotel room and seemed to be in a big hurry to leave the group. So John put all her luggage in the trunk of the old car that had brought her there and said his good-byes to the people who would be gone when he came back. To be honest, he would have preferred kitchen duty. But Juliette was his sister and his responsibility. Colette joined him in the car, and they drove silently to the nearest town where John's sister would be able to board a vessel heading for Paris. Once they had parked in front of the Dol de Bretagne train station, they took out the heavy monsters his sister called suitcases and walked to the platform to wait for the train. John's sister looked once again as if she had bit into a lemon. The smiles and good humor of the previous day were definitely gone. Thankfully, after a very long minute, the steam engine arrived, and John was able to put all the offending bags in the car his sister was going to travel in. And as the train controller announced the impending departure, John awkwardly hugged her good-bye. Colette followed his lead.

But as Colette drew near, her sister-in-law pulled her closer and whispered, "I have a message from my mother. She asked me to tell you that you may have won this battle…but not the war."

About the author

Michelina Vinter is a practicing acupuncturist and herbalist residing in the San Francisco Bay area with her two children, her husband, and a sweet little shadow, her son's Havanese. Possessing a vivid imagination since she was a child, she often was told to get to the point—which led to her career as an acupuncturist. Born in France, she left her family and moved to the United States when she was twelve years old. With firsthand experiences in hard goodbyes and long conversations with her maternal grandmother who was born in 1920, Vinter's wisdom beyond her years has led to a fulfilling writing career covering multiple genres.